Aviary

Emily A. Steward

Azure Sky

Aviary by Emily A. Steward

Cover art by Chad Steward

This is a work of fiction. Names, places, characters, and events are fictitious in every regard. Any similarities to actual events and persons, living or dead, are purely coincidental. Any trademarks, service marks, product names, or named features are assumed to be the property of their respective owners, and are used only for reference. There is no implied endorsement if any of these terms are used.

Except for review purposes, the reproduction of this book in whole or part, electronically or mechanically, constitutes a copyright violation.

AVIARY

Copyright © 2024 EMILY A. STEWARD

*To my husband Chad,
whose amazing art has graced each of my books.
Thank you for all your hard work. We make an awesome team!
Also, to my brothers Jeremy and Jameson,
who have joined me on many crazy adventures in the woods when
we were kids, building tree forts and searching for monsters.*

Table of Contents

Chapter One 1
Chapter Two 14
Chapter Three 25
Chapter Four 36
Chapter Five 52
Chapter Six 64
Chapter Seven 88
Chapter Eight 94
Chapter Nine 105
Chapter Ten 126
Chapter Eleven 137
Chapter Twelve 146
Chapter Thirteen 159
Chapter Fourteen 163
Chapter Fifteen 173
Chapter Sixteen 182
Chapter Seventeen 190
Chapter Eighteen 198
Chapter Nineteen 207
Chapter Twenty 230
About the Author 244
About the Artist 245

Chapter One

Tam watched the young trainees from her perch in the tree as they practiced in groups of two on the platform below. Each held a wooden sword as they circled each other, striking out while doing their best to avoid their opponent. She longed to join in, but her father thought it was too dangerous. *He thinks everything is too dangerous,* Tam thought with a scowl.

Sighing, she leaned forward, brushing aside the few strands of auburn hair falling out of her braid. Several of the students had begun chopping hay bales with sharpened shokas. The design of a shoka allowed for the chopping power of an axe, and the stabbing power of a spear. It was one of the standard weapons for all Pathfinders. Others put on their tree climbing equipment to practice their climbing and jumps. It was all in preparation for the Pathfinder test.

The test was often brutal. Tam shivered as she remembered the broken bones and bloody faces of the challengers from last year. But the test was far less brutal than having someone unskilled go up against the enormous wild boars, known as the kapros, that stalked the forest floor below. Only the elite few were strong enough to face them, and only those that proved themselves during the test would become Pathfinders. Rolling up her sleeves, she flexed her arm and frowned. Tam ran her fingers over her bicep, hoping to feel a bulging muscle hiding beneath the surface. No luck.

Continuing to watch, she recognized a few faces from Sparrow and Raven district, but most of the kids were from the stronger tribes, Hawk and Falcon.

Tam loved the trees in her forest home, but she was growing weary of the same scenery every day. No one in the entire village ever dared set foot on the ground. Well, no one except the Pathfinders.

Hendrik, one of the boys she knew from Sparrow tribe, chopped a haybale in half in one fluid motion. He wiped his brow then spotted Tam in the tree. Instantly, a crooked smile broke out on his face, and he slung the shoka over his shoulder. Tam groaned. He'd always been a bit of a showoff, parading around like a peacock in front of the girls and expecting them to swoon over him.

"Hey, Sticks!" he called up with a flirtatious wink.

Grimacing at the unfortunate nickname, she rubbed her thin arms and looked away. Hendrik was one of most skilled and promising of the young men in their tribe, and he knew it. He also thought any girl, including Tam, should be overjoyed if he showed an interest in them. She wasn't.

"Hi there!" came an unfamiliar voice.

Tam jumped. The face of a young girl appeared just below her. The tree climbing claws she had strapped to her wrists dug deep into the bark. These contraptions helped provide the extra grip Pathfinders needed to cling to the sides of trees.

"Um, hi."

"Mind if I join you and roost here awhile? I could use a rest."

Before Tam could answer, the girl had scrambled up the rest of the way and plopped down next to her among the large boughs. "I'm Willow," she said.

"Tam. From Sparrow tribe."

Willow grabbed her hand and shook it vigorously, a huge smile on her face. "I'm from Raven tribe." The girl was a tiny thing. Her short, cropped hair matched her bird-like energy.

"Aren't you a little young to be a Pathfinder? I thought you had to be sixteen."

"Don't let my size fool you," Willow said with a wink. "I'm no nestling. I turned seventeen last month."

Tam shook her head. She could hardly believe this petite girl sitting beside her was a year older than her.

Willow tilted her head to the side, looking more like a bird than ever. "Why aren't you down there training?"

"Oh, I'm not a trainee. At least not a Pathfinder trainee. My dad wants me to be a Keeper," Tam said with a sigh. She used to enjoy taking care of the birds that helped supply the city with fresh meat, but it was always the same thing, day in and day out, and she wanted adventure and excitement.

"Don't you want to be one?"

"No, but according to my dad, it's my only choice. He believes those of us from Sparrow tribe should stick to farming and agriculture and become Keepers. He says I should leave the dangerous work to the stronger tribes."

Willow nodded. "I get that. I come from a family of Pathfinders, and I can tell you, they don't have the highest life expectancy."

"A family of Pathfinders? That's pretty rare for Raven, isn't it?"

"Yes, we just aren't cut out to be merchants or scribes like most Ravens. Not enough excitement. It's a dangerous job though. My dad died during a mission before I was born."

"Oh, I'm sorry. My mom is dead too, even though she was trained as a Keeper. Died when I was a baby. It was during the big earthquake while trying to keep the birds from escaping from the damaged net. An aftershock took her by surprise, and she fell."

Willow sighed and shook her head. "I guess being a Pathfinder isn't the only dangerous job. Still, one of my aunts and two of my uncles were also killed while on missions." She plucked a leaf from the tree and tore it into smaller pieces, staring into the distance at nothing in particular.

"By the kapros?" Tam raised her eyebrows. The giant boar made her shiver both with excitement and fear. She'd never seen one up close before.

"Yeah. Well ... kind of. One of my uncles fell from a tree when he misjudged the distance of a jump. Fell straight down just like a widow maker."

"A widow maker?"

"Yeah, you know. Like a dead branch. Sorry, I guess that's Pathfinder lingo."

"Stevens, get back down here!" a trainer with a limp yelled up to Willow. "This is no time for socialization."

Dropping the remains of the ripped-up leaf, Willow brushed off her hands on her pants and shrugged. "I better go. See you around."

"Yeah, see you."

"And good luck learning to be a Keeper!" she called back and sprang to nearby tree.

"Good luck becoming a ..." Tam's voice trailed off as she watched the other girl climb expertly from tree to tree, sticking her tree claws into the bark and swinging down to join the others. She exhaled. "Wow."

Tam longed to join them. To explore, go on adventures, glean food and supplies for the Colony, and fight kapros was her dream. Instead, she was stuck in the trees of Aviary never to see the outside world. All she could do was watch the others from afar. If only her father would let her train.

Her eyes darted to the sun. *Oh no! It's almost noon!* She had lost track of time. Dad was going to be so mad.

Climbing back down the way she'd come, Tam sped along the bridge toward home. She and her father lived right next to the bird farms, not far from the center of Aviary. She'd gotten up early and gone to the outskirts of the village to watch the training. Luckily, she knew all the shortcuts through the village, and it didn't take long for her to reach the zipline she and her friend, Elnor, had set up leading to the next platform. The line allowed her to skip a flight of stairs and several bridges. She sucked in her breath and jumped off the edge.

Tam never quite got used to the exhilaration of flying across the village with wind whipping all around her. It was frightening but wonderful. Even though Elnor had helped her make the zipline, she never could talk her into trying it out. Elnor was a bit of a powder down softie, though Tam would never tell her friend that. The platform was coming up fast. She brought her legs up and landed in a run, stumbling and stopping just inches from the rough bark of a tree. Regaining her balance, she raced past several people going about their day-to-day tasks. A few of them waved as they saw her dash by, and Tam smiled and nodded in their direction. Climbing the final ladder on the backside of their home, she arrived at the farm breathless.

"You're late, Tamarelda." Her dad was filling the water trough. He spoke without looking up. "I had to round up a clutch of a dozen blue myself for a shipment to Raven district."

Tam flinched more at the sound of her full name than his tone. She unlatched the netting, careful not to let any birds escape, and stepped inside the enclosure. "I'm sorry. Elnor and I got caught up in a game of ten tiles. It won't happen again."

Her dad set down the now empty can and dried his hands on his shirt. "Elnor came by looking for you less than an hour ago."

"Oh, well ... I—"

"Where were you?"

Tam swallowed and tried to think of another excuse. When nothing came, she blurted out the truth. "I wanted to watch the training."

Her father's eyes flashed. "You know I don't want you watching them, getting ideas in your head. Your job is here." He picked the can back up and walked to the shed, slamming the can on the shelf much harder than necessary.

"What's the big deal? I didn't think just watching could do any harm." Tam sat down on a bench. A blue jay swooped down, landing on her outstretched arm. Such a beautiful bird. It was a shame they had to be raised as food for the village, but with the kapros devouring every land animal in sight, they didn't have many options.

"I don't think you thought it over at all. There are young birds that need their food on time, as well as rips in the nets that need mending. If the rips were to grow too large, we could lose dozens of our flock. I don't think you grasp the importance of our job."

Frustrated, Tam sighed. "No, I do. It's just ..."

"Just what?" He scooped some seed from the bag in the shed and returned, throwing a handful of seeds into the air. The blue jay jumped from Tam's arm to join the other birds as they pecked the floor clean in a matter of seconds.

"It's just that ... Well, I don't want to be stuck in this job forever. I'm not a nestling anymore. I'm seventeen. I should be able to choose what to do with my life, and what I want is to be a Pathfinder."

"You're not seventeen yet," he said with a harrumph as he threw out another handful of seeds. "And it's far too dangerous. You know that. To see the kapros—"

"Is to see death," Tam finished, rolling her eyes. "I know, I know. But I would be careful. I'd be so careful." She stared up at the canopy of netting above them as birds dove down to join in the feast, filling the air with the sound of flapping wings.

"Besides it being dangerous, you're not built for it. It takes years of training. Some of those kids from Hawk and Falcon district have been practically training since infancy. You wouldn't be able to pass the test."

"That's not fair. Why should they get the advantage?"

"Tameraida, you know as well as I do they are the strongest districts."

Tam turned her head away and rolled her eyes. Here came the same old lecture about her proper place in the community.

"Nearly all the people from Hawk tribe become Constructors or Guardians because they are big and strong, and the strongest among them become Pathfinders. As for Falcon, their people are Craftsmen so they build the Pathfinder gear. Many of their youth grow up using the equipment and become skilled at the use of weaponry and climbing. This benefits them during the test. You need to stick with what you were made to do. Besides, being a Keeper is just as important. Someone needs to provide food for the village."

"Hendrik is going to take the test, and he's from Sparrow."

Her dad harrumphed, and his face grew red. "That is up to Hendrik's parents. They are not responsible for you. I am."

Well, can I at least try to train for the test with the others? If I don't pass, I'll drop it. I promise."

"No. I forbid you from training with them. You could get hurt, and there is no use getting your hopes up." Her dad dropped a feed bucket next to her. "Now, enclosure four still needs their food, and three needs mending on the top right of the cage."

She sighed and stood up. "All right. I'm going."

"Get a move on. They've waited long enough for their breakfast. Oh, and later tonight, I want you to visit your grandmother. She's still not feeling well."

Tam's grandmother was one of the oldest people in the village and was actually her great-grandmother, but Tam simply referred to her as her Gran. She'd outlived everyone who had any memory of what the world was like before the great wars and before the kapros had taken over the land. Sometimes Gran would tell stories about what life was like back then. Flying machines, small boxes that allowed you to talk to people miles away called phones, and huge indoor places you could buy anything you wanted. It was, however, sometimes difficult to tell fact from fiction.

Gran could be difficult to understand because her thoughts often flitted from one place to another, like starlings at play. At times, Gran thought she was a scientist in a lab; other times, the driver of something called an ice cream truck, and Tam would have to pretend to enjoy eating the invisible treats Gran would pass out. She'd been that way since Tam could remember, but she was kind and had a strong fondness for her great-granddaughter, even if she didn't always remember Tam's name.

Tam stopped at the house on her way to enclosure four, grabbed her brown backpack, and opened it to make sure her homemade tree claws, shoe spikes, and crude shoka were still inside.

Tam was quite proud of hers. She'd made it from a broomstick handle and placed a long spike at the tip and a butcher's knife underneath. Even the Craftsmen in Falcon District would be impressed. Smiling, Tam closed her bag and slung it over her shoulders. Dad may have forbidden her from training with the others, but he never said she couldn't train on her own.

After feeding the birds and mending the net, she set off to a remote corner of the village. Tam had learned a few things from watching the trainees that morning and was anxious to put them into practice. Bending down, she tied the spikes to her feet before putting on her tree claws. She took a deep breath and then sprang to the nearest tree, slamming her body into the side and gasping for breath. She would have to practice her jump a bit more. The spikes needed to slam into the tree, not her body. At least everything was holding well.

Yanking out her left spike, Tam stabbed it into the tree higher up, going hand over hand until she could reach the limb overhead, then hoisted herself up, already breathless. Even though she'd been practicing since the test last year, it was still physically draining. The next tree was over open ground with no platform to catch her if she fell. Tam had never gone away from the platform before, but the test was coming up quickly, and if she didn't get over her fear of falling, she'd never be a Pathfinder. What had Willow called it? Falling like a widow maker? That made it sound even worse.

The other tree had a limb a little lower. If Tam ran and jumped from the limb, she should be able to make it easily. Peering down at the forest floor, she nodded with satisfaction. No kapros in sight.

Tam took a few breaths to settle her nerves, then took a running leap, taking care to keep her arms and legs in front of her and landed perfectly. This was even more exhilarating than the zipline. She climbed and jumped again and again, fully enjoying the feeling. This was amazing! After a while, it began to feel natural. Could she be good at this after all? A dead tree was to her right. Tam leapt to it just like the others. Her spikes made a hollow sound as they struck, sinking in deep. The tree shook and, to her horror, began to fall sideways. Out of instinct, she leapt for another tree as the dead timber crashed into some branches, but her claws didn't strike it hard enough and the spikes slid down the trunk, not finding purchase. Tam leapt for a branch, but her momentum tore her fingers from it. Her heart leapt to her throat as she tumbled toward the ground, arms flailing.

Tam landed flat on her back with a thud. The forest was silent except for the wind rustling the leaves overhead.

Gasping for breath, she wiggled her fingers and toes to make sure everything was still intact. Moving her hands, she felt the earth underneath her. It was pleasantly warm from the sun and grainy. So, this was what the ground felt like. The scent of the soil filled her nostrils, sweet and refreshing. Sitting up, she looked herself over. Despite a few scratches, she seemed okay. Looking down at the brown dirt beneath her in awe, Tam got to her knees and scooped up a pile and let it run through the cracks between her fingers. It was soft, damp, and left a pleasant residue on her palms. She took a deep breath, enjoying the smell. They had soil in the gardens from composting, but this was real, wild dirt. It felt different somehow. It was filled with small, hard objects. These must be stones. She just had to take some of it with her. With a smile, Tam gathered it up by the handful and stuffed it in her pockets.

A loud snort came from close by. Too close. The sound sent chills down her arms and neck. Slowly, she raised her head. No more than three feet away, a massive kapros towered in front of her.

Chapter Two

The thick fur covering the boar was dark and matted. Drool dripped from tusks that were longer than Tam's arm. The creature's breathing came in heaves. Tam could feel the warmth from where she knelt, stunned. Another grunt from the creature made her scurry backward. The creature lowered its head, preparing to charge and rip her to shreds. Her body was almost even with a big tree now. If she could only make it back a little further.

Tam gasped as the kapros rushed forward. She just managed to dive behind the tree at the last second. The animal grazed the tree, making the whole thing shake. The kapros rounded on her faster than seemed possible. Before she could stand, it came at her again. She moved to the side just enough for the two tusks to dig into the bark around her stomach, pinning her between them. The impact dislodged the dead tree that had been stuck in the branches overhead. A horrible screech echoed through the forest as the dead timber fell on top of the boar, tearing his tusks away from the tree.

Tam took this moment to stand and jump to the highest branch within reach. The kapros knocked the dead log to the side as if it were nothing. It splintered to pieces as it struck another tree. It came at her again, missing her feet by inches as she scrambled upward, heart racing. Her whole body was weak and wobbly, and her arms could barely hang on from shaking. The tree rattled as the kapros rammed into it. Tam's grip slipped, and she slid toward the beast, clawing and reaching for anything to stop her descent. Her scream reverberated through the forest. A sharp, searing pain in her calf made her gasp as something dug into her flesh.

With all her strength, she jumped for the branches overhead, trying to swing herself up, but the branch snapped, catapulting her down a ravine. Tam yelped as brambles tore at her arms and legs as she rolled, finally coming to a stop near a stream. Climbing to her feet, she raced along the ground as fast as her spinning head would let her and dove behind a large boulder. Tam paused to catch her breath. Her chest heaved in and out as she listened for the creature to come barreling after her. The thunderous noise left no doubt. It was coming.

Tam searched the area for an escape route, but all the trees nearby were too short. A loud snort brought her attention down to the bushes in front of her as the kapros stepped out. How had it gotten in front of her? *No, No, No. It can't end like this.* The boar smelled the air before locking its eyes on her. But this boar was different. It had a bushier mane and flecks of white on its scarred snout. *Another one?* Tam swallowed, her mouth so dry it caused her to choke and cough.

The kapros charged forward, and Tam screamed, flattening herself against the boulder, but before it could reach her, something slammed into its side. The other kapros had arrived, and it had no intention of sharing its meal. Tam froze, watching them go at it. The second boar regained his footing and chomped down on the first. He let out a shrill squeal and reared up, coming down on the other with his hooves.

Tam shook her head, coming to her senses. As they fought, she crawled along the ground and into the brush. Laying quietly with her heart pounding, Tam listened to the sounds of the feral pigs thrashing around behind her. This was it. It was her chance to escape unnoticed, and she had to take it. With renewed energy, Tam got to her feet and sprinted toward the tree line. Were they following her? She didn't take the time to see and, instead, swung herself up into the branches of a tall oak and kept climbing upward until she was about fifty feet off the ground. Almost as high as her forest home. Confidant this was enough to keep a safe distance above the kapros vision, Tam jumped to the next tree and the next until the sounds of the battle were well behind her. Only then did she stop to examine the dull ache in her calf.

Her pant leg had been shredded up to her knee, and an angry gash dripped bright red blood. Knowing kapros were attracted to the scent of blood, she took a moment to rip off the torn part of her pants and wrap it around the wound to keep it from dripping, wincing. How was she going to explain this injury to her dad? It would have to stay hidden. With her leg bandaged, Tam made her way back to the colony. Slower now, still shaking from her close encounter. Finally, the colony came into view. Climbing up another twenty to thirty feet, she leapt onto the closest platform and made her way home, breathing hard and doing her best to hide any sort of limp in case anyone should see her.

When Tam stumbled through the door of her hut, her shirt was drenched with sweat. After scanning the room for her father, she tiptoed up the steps to her bedroom on the next platform and drew her curtains across the doorway. Tam tore off her clothes and hid them under her bed. If her dad saw her covered in dirt or the gash on her leg, he'd know something was up. She splashed water on her face from the basin in her room. *To see the kapros is to see death.* The quote her father was fond of saying suddenly took on a whole new meaning. Tam had looked death in the eye and felt its breath on her face. Sitting down on the edge of her cot, she shivered and rubbed her arms.

"Tamerelda, are you in here?"

Tam kicked her pants the rest of the way under the bed and grabbed some clothes from her drawer. "Just a minute." Once she was dressed, she pulled the curtain aside. "Yes?"

"I told you to look in on Gran after you got home today. She's been asking for you."

Tam nodded. "Right, sorry. I'll go see her now."

Her dad put his hand on her shoulder and raised her chin. "Are you feeling okay? You look a little pale. And are you limping?"

She pushed his hand aside, her breath catching in her throat. "I'm fine. I … uh, I just haven't eaten in a while, and I stubbed my toe on my bed."

He studied her for a moment. "Well, I'm making soup. After you visit Gran, it should be ready."

Tam went outside, climbed the stairs leading up to Gran's private house on an upper level, and rapped on the outside.

"Come in," came a faint voice.

The room was sparse. A rocking chair, wardrobe, and small bed were the only furniture. Her great-grandmother had her quilt pulled up to her chin. She smiled seeing Tam. "Did you bring soup? William said he was bringing soup." Her words came out wheezy. The effort seemed to irritate her throat, making her cough.

"No, William, er … Dad is still making it. How are you feeling?"

"The roses look lovely, don't they?" she asked, holding out a bunched-up handkerchief.

Tam sat in the rocker and pulled it close to the bed. "Yes, they look really nice."

"They smell good, too." The old woman shoved the hanky under Tam's nose. "Smell it."

She cupped her hand around the cloth and politely pretended to sniff it. "Smells great."

Gran's other hand shot out, grabbing Tam by the wrist. "Your hands ..." She dropped the handkerchief and pulled her granddaughter's hand closer. "You have dirt under your nails." Her Gran sniffed the air and straightened, her back rigid. "This is wild dirt." Staring at Tam, her eyes grew wide with fear. "You ... you've seen them, haven't you?"

"No, I—" Tam squirmed under her surprisingly strong grip. "Gran, you're hurting me."

"Too see the kapros is to see death! When your mother died, we swore we'd keep you away, so you wouldn't meet the same fate."

"My mother? But she died in the earthquake. What do you mean?"

Gran dropped her wrist. And sat back against her pillows. "Don't the roses look lovely today?" She scooped up the handkerchief again. "I must put them in water. Can you get me some water?"

"But Gran, what did you mean? Did the kapros have something to do with my mom's death?"

Gran glanced up at Tam, then back to the imaginary flowers and waved her question away. "I ... I need a vase. Yes, a vase."

A rap came at the door. Her father walked in, holding a tray with soup and a glass of water. Gran clapped her hands together. "Wonderful! Just what I need." Her features relaxed as she grabbed up the glass of water and shoved the handkerchief inside. "That should keep my roses fresh."

Tam slipped out while her father tried to convince Gran to drink some of her plant's water. She took a bowl of soup to her room and went to the basin and scrubbed at the dirt under her nails until her fingers were red, then sat down on her cot, sipping absently at the broth. Was Gran completely rambling, or was Dad hiding something from her? Had Mom really been killed by one of those things? But what reason did he have to lie? Gran didn't even know what day it was. She probably shouldn't take anything the woman said too seriously. Setting the half-finished bowl aside, she laid back, staring at the thatched ceiling.

She heard Dad's footsteps on the stairs and turned away from the door, drawing up her blanket and closing her eyes. The curtain rustled as he looked in.

"You asleep already?"

When Tam didn't respond, he let the curtain fall. Soon, the sound of him putting away dishes in the cupboard drifted upstairs. She needed to know if he was hiding something about Mom, but after her day, she just felt too exhausted. Besides, Gran said strange things all the time. It probably didn't mean anything. But on the other hand, Gran had never looked so frightened before.

As she waited for her body to relax and sleep to come, her mind wandered. Very few memories remained of her mother, and most of them were filled with more feelings than details. One in particular did stand out, however. A memory of being carried in a sling with the wind blowing on her face, birds chirping, her mother smiling down on her, and the scent of lavender all around. So peaceful. Sometimes, when Tam felt scared or sad, she would close her eyes and try to bring back that feeling of comfort and peace. She tried to force herself back to that memory now, but peace wouldn't come. Visions of the kapros kept popping into her head. Was she crazy to want to be a Pathfinder? Just thinking of how massive and vicious they had been made her heart pound even in the sanctuary of her room. But thinking of a lifetime as a Keeper being trapped in one place, never able to see wild vegetation and explore new places, scared her even more.

She'd read books about the world outside her little bubble. At least about how the world used to be. Back when people could freely walk on the ground. How amazing would that be? They lived in large cities made of metal and concrete and rode around in fast contraptions on wheels. The old world fascinated her. Tam's friend Elnore had an uncle that was a Pathfinder, and according to her, he'd seen many of the things from the old world firsthand during supply runs. She couldn't wait to see them too.

It had been a close call for sure, but she had survived. She'd seen a kapros and not seen death. Reaching under her bed, Tam pulled out the pants from earlier. The pockets still bulged with soil. Grabbing out a handful, she put it into a leather pouch, letting it run between her fingers as it fell. Tam would see the ground again and would become a Pathfinder. The test was the day after tomorrow, and she would be ready.

The next day, Tam finished her work early and set off with her practice gear in her bag. She was walking past the main hall when she saw Hendrik leaning against a railing. They made eye contact, and she immediately regretted it.

"Sticks, hi! Where are you going in such a hurry?"

Tam kept her eyes down and continued walking. "I'm just … I'm meeting a friend.

"Oh yeah, who?" Hendrik asked, falling in step beside her.

"Not that it's any of your business, but I'm meeting Elnor."

"Does Elnor know? Because her mom said she's sick with the flu or something."

"Oh." Tam scrunched up her nose. She had to quit using that girl as an alibi.

"So where are you really going?"

"Look, none of your business okay? Today is the last day, and I—" Tam blinked. She'd said too much.

Hendrik blocked her path. "Last day for what?" A look of realization dawned on him. "Are you going to take the test tomorrow?"

"What? No way. You're crazy. Move out of my way."

"You are!"

Tam pushed him aside. "So, what if I am? Are you going to tell your buddies and get a good laugh?"

Hendrik trotted to catch up to her. "No, I think it's great. Only ..."

Tam stopped. "Only what?"

"Only you haven't been training with us. I assume you've been training alone?"

"So what if I have?" Tam responded.

"To help your chances, you really should get an inside perspective. Someone to give you a different point of view and to help you know what to expect."

With a sigh, Tam's eyes met his. Was he making a serious offer to help or teasing? There was no hint of sarcasm in his voice, and his eyes seemed sincere. She knew she'd regret this, but he was right. She needed all the help she could get. "And I suppose you have someone in mind? Someone really skilled who can give me this heightened point of view you're talking about?"

Hendrik got a big dopey grin on his face. One that showed his annoying dimples. "Yeah, me!"

Chapter Three

Hendrik turned out to be a pretty good teacher. He took Tam to an old practice site that they didn't use anymore and showed her a few dodging techniques. The ground roll gave her a painful bruise on her shoulder, but after a few tries and suggestions from Hendrik, she soon had it mastered.

Hendrik pulled a log full of gashes in front of her. "Now, let's see your chopping power."

Tam pulled out her rusty blade.

"You won't get far with that thing," he said, handing her his own shoka. "Try this one."

Tam took the weapon and stood above the log.

Hendrick paced in front of her. "Now, aim counts just as much as chopping power during the test. Try to aim for this line." He ran his finger over a ridge.

She readied herself, staring hard at the line. Raising the shoka above her head, Tam brought it down with all her might. It bounced to the side, sending a tremor up her arms.

Hendrik laughed. "You need to keep a firm grip. Also, did you close your eyes?"

"What? No, I ... Maybe. Shut up."

Hendrik held his hands up. "Sorry, just trying to help. Try again. This time, firm grip, eyes open."

"Right." Tam nodded. She lifted the blade again, this time focusing on her grip, and brought it down hard. It landed with a satisfying clunk, deep into the wood. She smiled. "How about that?'

"Much better, but you still missed the line by a mile."

Tam sighed. "Like you can do better?"

Hendrik pulled the blade from the log, glanced down at the line, and brought it down with such force, the log broke in two.

"Wow." Tam blinked. "Still missed the mark though."

"What? Really?" He examined the log. The cut he'd made had missed the ridge by a full two inches. "Well … I didn't want you to feel too bad about yourself." Hendrik winked.

"Right." Tam scoffed.

"Do you have tree climbers?"

She pulled out her homemade gear and handed them to Hendrik.

"Those probably don't retract to allow you to grip limbs easily, right?"

Tam shook her head.

"Better than nothing, I suppose. Let's see what you can do."

He watched as Tam scaled the tree and made a few jumps. "Try to let the gear receive the brunt of the impact," he called.

"Bend your knees and elbows. That's it! Not bad for homemade gear. Not bad at all."

Tam dropped back down, panting. "Thanks. Don't you need to practice too?"

"Yeah, but we're not meeting 'til after lunch."

Tam looked at the sky. "It's nearly two o'clock."

"Oh, tree sap! I gotta go. See ya tomorrow!" Hendrik turned and started to sprint without waiting for a reply.

Maybe Hendrik wasn't such a jerk after all.

He turned around and gave her a wink as he ran.

She rolled her eyes. Maybe.

Looking down, she noticed one of her climbing claws was falling apart again. She'd fixed it several times in the past but needed some more rope to do it properly. With a sigh, Tam shoved her stuff in her bag and made her way back home.

That night, she tossed and turned, too nervous and excited to sleep. After counting the knotholes on her ceiling for the tenth time, Tam decided she might sleep better with a full stomach. She recoiled as her bare feet touched the cold floor, then eased them back down and soundlessly padded to the kitchen. Pulling some berry preserves out of the cupboard, she spread it on a piece of bread.

"Tamerelda, is that you?" came her Dad's hoarse voice from the stairs.

"Yeah, it's me." She turned to see him standing at the foot of the stairs with the branch in his hand he kept by the bed in case of an intruder. Not that anyone in the colony would break into their house, but he was a cautious man.

"Oh good." Dad set down his crude weapon and sat next to her at the table. "Can't sleep, huh?"

Tam picked at the bread. "Nope. Sorry to wake you."

"You didn't wake me. I couldn't sleep either. I guess it's just that kind of night. Must be the humidity." He paused a moment, shifting his weight in the chair. "Listen, I hope you aren't upset about not being able to take the test tomorrow. You're just so young, and I ... Well, your place is here. Besides, I'd hate to lose you too."

Tam bit her lip. Did she dare ask about Mom? Glancing up at him, Tam made up her mind. "You said Mom died during the earthquake, right?"

"That's right." He cleared his throat. "Why do you ask?"

"Well, Gran seems to think she was killed by a kapros. Why is that?"

Dad's face flushed. "You know your grandma. Always saying all kinds of things. Her mind is going. She's not living in reality."

"Is this one true?"

Her father stood up. "Don't you think it's time to get some rest?"

"Dad?"

He let out a deep breath, then sat back down. "Yes. Yes, it's true."

Tam's head spun. She was thankful she was already sitting down. "Then why did you tell me Mom was killed by the earthquake?"

"I said she was killed during the earthquake, not by it."

"How? Did she fall and they trampled her?"

"This isn't the time, Tam. It's late."

Tam clenched her fist. "When is the time then?"

When he spoke again, his voice had an edge to it. Deep and husky. "I said I don't want to discuss it."

"You can't keep treating me like a child. I have the right to know, and I have the right to do what I want with my own life."

When he didn't respond, Tam sprang from her chair. "Dad, I'm taking that test tomorrow. I don't care what you say."

"Enough!" He slammed his fist down on the counter, making the dishes rattle. She'd certainly bent his feathers. "The kapros took everything from me. I'll not let them have you too."

Tam pushed her chair back and got to her feet. "I'm taking the test. The village rules state that anyone sixteen and up should be allowed to participate. I'm going."

Her father's eyes grew wide with fury, and his face reddened. She'd never seen him more furious. He looked like he was about to say something else, but the whistle of the kettle cut him off.

"Your coffee is ready," Tam said before stomping up to her room. She half expected him to come up after her, but he didn't follow. Tam peeked out of the curtain an hour later and saw him sitting at the kitchen table, slowly sipping his coffee. She was fed up with him treating her like a prisoner. And why did he refuse to talk about Mom's death? If she was still alive, Mom would surely support her dreams. She wouldn't try to keep her trapped like an animal. Dad was just paranoid and selfish to keep her here. Tam narrowed her eyes, more determined than ever to pass the test tomorrow. That's what Mom would have wanted. She had to do well. Not only for herself but for her mother. Her death deserved to be avenged, and Tam was the only one who could do it.

Dad wasn't home when she woke the next morning. After eating a quick breakfast and packing her bag, Tam set off to do her morning rounds. To her surprise, all the work had already been done. Her dad must have gotten up at the crack of dawn to get it all finished so fast. Maybe he couldn't sleep. A pang of guilt washed over her. Should she apologize? No, he was the one being unreasonable. She kept expecting to see him at one of the enclosures, but he was nowhere in sight.

It was a little early, but she decided to head off to the testing grounds. Hopefully she could make good time and settle in while waiting for everyone to arrive. Once checked in, she was sure the knot in her stomach would lessen.

"Off to watch the Pathfinder test today?" Mr. Brown, the baker, asked as she walked by his hut.

Tam nodded. "Have you seen my dad around?"

"Not today, sorry. Leaving a little early, aren't you? The test doesn't start for another hour."

"Just want to get a good spot."

"Good idea. The whole colony is going to be there."

Tam's stomach chose that moment to rebel against the oats she'd had for breakfast, and it let out a groan. She crossed her arms over her stomach to muffle the sound. "The whole colony?"

"Yep. Should be a good crowd. Everyone likes to get a little view of the excitement and the violence," he added with a wink. "Wonder how many bones will be broken this year? I have a bet riding on five."

Tam swallowed and adjusted the strap from her bag on her shoulder. Her mouth was suddenly dry.

"Anyway, see you there! I'm going to finish up here and head out soon."

She nodded. "Yeah, see you there."

When she finally arrived at the testing grounds, the seats really were already filling up. A few people in the stands recognized Tam and were pointing and waving. Elnor was there with her entire family.

"Tam!" Elnor shouted. "Saved you a seat!" Tam shook her head and pointed to the registration desk. Elnor's eyes went wide. Tam loved her friend, but honestly, sometimes she could be a little slow. Why did she think Tam had been training for the last year?

As she walked over to a table where a woman with a sharp nose was getting people registered, she spotted Hendrik. He nodded at her, then said something to his buddies. They all looked her way and laughed.

Tam's face burned. It stung even more since just yesterday he had pretended to be her friend. He probably told them all about her homemade equipment and clumsiness. She hadn't misjudged him after all and wanted to wipe that smug grin of his face with her fist. Such an immature crop drinker. Glaring back at them, she moved to the front of the line. After giving her name, the woman at the table raised an eyebrow.

"Johansson you say?"

Tam nodded. "Yes, ma'am."

"Very interesting." The woman pursed her lips but said nothing more before handing Tam a number to pin on her shirt. Number twenty-four. That meant that so far there were twenty-three others trying out this year, and more were lined up behind her. She knew from previous years only a small percentage would qualify. What were the chances she'd be one of them? No, she couldn't afford to think like that, and she wasn't going to let herself chicken out now.

Tam walked by a line of Pathfinders. They were all geared up in brown uniforms with grapplers attached to their waist and a shoka sheathed at their side. Tam couldn't wait to join them someday. The men and women stood at attention, not moving an inch. They looked so cool. Could she ever look like that? So calm, collected, and hardcore? It gave her a shiver of excitement to picture herself standing next to them. Even General Kaan was there. His dark beard had traces of silver hair, making him look quite distinguished. Tam hoped she didn't make a fool of herself in front of the leader of the Pathfinders.

She leaned against the rope railing separating the observers from the trainees and snuck glances at the competitors. Most of them were close to her age, but a few looked like they were in their twenties and one man looked closer to fifty. Some of the trainees were much bigger than she was. One boy had taken his shirt off and was flexing his muscles. What a showoff. She rolled her eyes and looked away, then allowed herself one more glance.

"He's pretty cute, isn't he?"

Tam jumped. "Huh?" Willow, the girl she'd met while watching training stood next to her. The other girl's head only came to Tam's shoulder. "Oh, hi." Tam's face flushed. That girl sure had a way of sneaking up on her.

"His name is Dover, and he's from Hawk tribe. He's talented. I'd be shocked if he didn't pass." Willow scrunched up her face. "Hey, I thought you weren't training. I thought you were going to be a Keeper."

"Yeah, well so did my dad. He's not too happy with me right now." Tam's shoulders slumped. "I haven't even seen him today."

"Wow." She let out a low whistle. "Maybe he just needs a little time. He'll come around."

Tam doubted it. Willow hadn't seen her dad's face last night. "Yeah, maybe."

"Want some berries?" She held out a handful of blue fruit.

Tam shook her head, nauseous at the thought.

"Suit yourself," Willow said, taking another mouthful.

A blond girl with her hair pulled back in a tight braid approached them. She was tall, lean, and wore brown shorts and a white tank top that showed off her toned biceps.

"Tam, this is Grace from Falcon district," Willow said. "We're training partners."

"Hi," Tam said. "Nice to meet you. I'm from Sparrow."

"Sparrow?" Grace scoffed, then leaned against a tree, spinning her shoka from hand to hand and acting quite bored. "It looks like all the tribes are represented this year. Raven, Hawk, Falcon, and Sparrow. I honestly don't know why they bother. We all know only Hawk and Falcon are going to make it through. Well, except you of course, Willow, but you're an exception. Most of them I recognize from training, but there are a few who must have had private teachers." She glanced sideways at Tam. "Did *you* have a private trainer?"

"No, I ... Well, Hendrik tried to help a little yesterday, but I've mainly been training on my own."

Grace raised her eyebrows. "Really?" A small smile formed at the corner of her mouth.

"What?"

"Nothing. I've just never heard of someone doing that before. I guess we'll see what you're made of soon. I'm sure the nestlings will be weeded out quickly."

"Tam will do great," Willow said with a grin. "She's special. I can tell." Grace scoffed, but Willow didn't seem to notice. "We better get geared up and ready. See you out there." She slapped Tam on the shoulder before following Grace toward the other trainees.

"Yeah, see you." Tam's hands trembled as she bent down and unzipped her pack. "Ah, man," she said under her breath. Tam had forgotten to fix her left tree claw. That was just great. She pulled it out and tried to wrap the broken strap back into place. It wasn't long enough to give it a proper tie off, but she did her best. That would just have to do. Even though the challenges changed every year, it was certain they would have to demonstrate climbing skills at some point.

"Attention, trainees!" Mayor Steadman held a crude megaphone and stood on a large podium made from logs. "Places, please. The first challenge is about to begin."

Chapter Four

Tam stood facing the podium with the others, waiting for further instruction.

"The test will be comprised of two parts," Steadman continued. "Each round is designed to test different crucial abilities you will need to become a Pathfinder. Round one will test your strength and combat skills, and round two will test your agility and speed."

Tam took a deep breath. This was getting very real. She shifted her weight and glanced at the other competitors' faces. Some looked as nervous as she was too; others were determined and fierce. She tried to match their intimidating scowls.

"You okay? Willow asked. "You look like you're going to be sick or something."

Tam pursed her lips. Not quite the look she was going for. Tam waved the other girl away. "I'm fine, just trying to keep myself focused."

"Well, you look more like you're constipated. Loosen up, or you're going to tense and freeze. You need to stay limber."

"Limber, got it." She shook her arms and wrists, trying to shake off her case of nerves.

The mayor read the first name on his list. "Dover of Hawk tribe, you will be first up." He directed the muscle bound, shirtless boy to the center of the platform.

Tam and the others watched from the sidelines. It gave her a little satisfaction seeing how nervous Hendrik seemed. He kept pacing and biting his fingernails. Not so cool and collected now. He caught her eye and stopped pacing to flash a grin and give her a wink. She groaned. Same old Hendrik.

"Today you will all be facing your very own kapros," Mayor Steadman announced. Gasps rippled through the crowd. The trainees standing in the center of the platform looked from side-to-side, as if expecting a kapros to spring from the trees. Steadman cleared his throat. "Not to worry. These kapros are manmade." He pointed to the far side of the arena. Tam squinted. The trees had huge logs suspended between them by long ropes. Several men wheeled out a log so it could be seen close up. It had been hollowed out, then carved to loosely resemble a kapros, including stout legs, tusks, and some hay to simulate the fur.

The mayor came down and stood next to the wooden boar. It was taller than he was and three times as wide. "As many of you know, there are two main areas Pathfinders strike in order to take kapros down," he said. "For the benefit of those watching, I will give a brief explanation. These hogs have developed a particularly thick hide. We have discovered through much trial and error and lives lost, small areas of weakness. These spots allow Pathfinders to reach vital areas of the animal such as the heart, lungs, and spinal column.

"If you will notice, beneath the front legs just at the armpit of each kapros, you will find a small red target. Your shoka should be plunged up at a slight angle toward the center of the animal to assure you hit a vital area such as the heart or lungs. The wood in this part of the body has been made with a softer material.

"On top, you will also find a red line on the back of the neck about two inches wide. This represents the spot you must slice through in order to sever the spinal column. This area is not as soft as the armpit, and much strength and technique will have to be employed to make the cut. Using your shoka, you must either stab the animal through the heart or chop deep into the neck, precisely on the line. The blade must sink at least three inches into the heart or neck for it to be counted."

Tam ran her finger over the dull blade she had with her. Would it be able to do the job?

"Kapros in the wild won't just stand there waiting for you to make your move, and neither will these. Each log will swing toward you with incredible speed and force, just as wild kapros would. Any questions?"

The trainees looked a little uneasy at the thought of an enormous log swinging directly at them. Willow raised her hand. "How long do we have to make the kill?"

"You will have three swings to eliminate the boar, and that is much more time than a live one will give you. Now, ready yourself," he said to Dover. The boy nodded and took a wide stance, holding the blade of his shoka in front of him.

Mayor Steadman lifted his arm. When he brought it down, they released the giant log. It raced toward him, faster than Tam had imagined. Dover's face was expressionless. He didn't waver as the object got closer. Tam took a deep breath and held it. Dover still hadn't moved. He was going to be crushed. Just as the log was about to plow into him, he stepped to the side and with one fluid motion, grabbed the log and casually swung himself on top of it. He stood and, while keeping his balance, swung the shoka down with all his might. The entire blade disappeared as it sank deep into the wood. He leapt from the log and landed in a roll. The spectators cheered, including the other trainees. "Well that didn't look so hard," a boy to Tam's left commented.

But it was more difficult than Dover made it look. The next five trainees who tried Dover's technique failed horribly. Only one of them managed to get astride the wooden boar, and he couldn't get his blade to cut deep enough before he fell off. The boy limped away with his head down, a look of defeat on his features.

They called Willow next. Tam was so nervous for her new friend that she almost forgot to be anxious for herself.

Willow stood at the line with her feet planted apart, and her shoka held in front of her.

"Ready?" Steadman asked.

She gave a slight nod. The log was released, hurtling toward her small frame. Willow narrowed her eyes. Tam's heart thumped in her ears as they all watched. Willow waited until the log was about to strike, then leaned to the side and back, taking advantage of her short stature. Tam gasped as the log whisked just over the other girl's face. She straightened back up and turned. Blood dripped from a shallow scratch on her cheek, but she ignored it and planted her feet again, waiting for the wooden boar to swing back. It didn't take long to close the distance. Willow leaned back again, but this time thrust her weapon out in front of her at the same time. The girl let go the instant it connected. The log swung away with her shoka firmly planted in the target area. Willow came over and stood next to Tam as the judges examined the blow.

Tam patted her shoulder. "Great job! That was amazing. Did you pass?"

"We'll see soon enough." Willow watched the judges pull out the shoka and examine the weapon and the wood. After a short huddle, Mayor Steadman announced, "Three and a half inches! Welcome to round two, number twelve!"

The crowd cheered, as Willow let out a sigh of relief.

"Next up, number ten, Polly Wattkins of Hawk tribe."

A girl about eighteen or nineteen took her place at the center. She planted her feet apart and gave a nod. The log rushed forward. The girl leaned back and to the side, trying to slip under as Willow had done while stabbing with her weapon. The weapon glanced off the wood, and the log plowed into the girl's upper torso, which had been only inches too high. Her shoulder made a horrible crunching sound as it connected with the unforgiving wood. She screamed at first, then lay on her back moaning. The log must have also clipped her head. Bright red blood streamed from her temple. The medics who'd been waiting on the sidelines ran to help. They asked her a few questions and examined her head before helping her sit up. Her arm hung limply at her side, and her shoulder protruded at a strange angle.

"Looks dislocated," Willow whispered.

Tam nodded. "Yeah, looks painful." The medics helped her gingerly onto a stretcher and took her to the medic tent set up beside the stands.

Steadman cleared his throat before speaking from the podium. "I'm sure Miss Watkins will be just fine. She's in good hands."

A scream came from the tent, echoing around the forest. Tam shivered. They must have put her arm back in place.

Steadman went on as if the scream hadn't happened. "Next up is number twenty-four, Tam Johansson of Sparrow tribe."

Tam took an involuntary step back. She wasn't ready and could feel the fear rising inside her chest as everyone waited for her to come forward. As she closed her eyes, images of Polly laying on the ground, bleeding from a headwound danced behind her eyelids.

"You can do this," she whispered to herself, trying to steady her breathing.

Willow gave her a reassuring smile. Grace said something to Hendrik and glanced at Tam's rusty shoka blade. Tam's eyes flashed. She had to rub that smug look of Grace's face. She'd show her. She'd show them both. Taking a deep breath, Tam jutted out her chin and strode forward, tripping over a loose board in her haste. She tried to catch herself but landed hard on her knees, face burning. Hendrik hurried over and extend a hand, but she ignored him and stood on her own, wincing and praying the gash on her leg hadn't reopened. The crowd murmured to one another. Tam scanned the audience. Elnor had her hand over her mouth, her brow furrowed in concern.

Her father's eyes locked on hers, and for a moment, she couldn't move. Was he right? Was this a horrible mistake? Grace snickered behind her, and her blush deepened and crept up to her ears.

"You've got this, Tam!" Willow shouted.

Tam tried to still her shaking hands. It was too late to turn back now. Standing up straight, she strode forward with as much dignity as possible, stopping at the line and holding her blade in front of her. Closing one eye, she aimed the tip of her blade at the log, getting ready to drop. Tam didn't trust herself to jump on top of the moving boar, but maybe if her timing was right, she could stab it in the heart and dodge to the side before it struck.

"Are you ready?" the mayor asked.

Ready? No. She wasn't ready, but she found herself nodding like an idiot all the same. Before she could give it a second thought, the log was released. It hurtled toward her faster than anticipated. Jumping out of the way, she landed hard on her elbow and winced. She'd barely had time to move much less stab it. Getting to her feet, Tam turned to face it again. The speed had slowed slightly, but it was still moving at an incredible rate. She moved to the side and stabbed with her blade as it went by, but her thrust was too soon, and Tam wasn't able to land a firm blow. The crowd collectively gasped as the shoka glanced off the wood and broke off in her hands.

No ... no, no, no! Tam stared in disbelief at the broken stick in her hand. The other half was on the floor near the loose board. She had no time and no weapon. Glancing down at the broken weapon, an idea came to her. Stomping on the boards, she heard a clunking sound. Several of these boards were loose.

She bent down and pulled. The board stuck a little at first, then bent back. The log was seconds away from its third and final sweep. Tam grabbed what was left of her weapon and wedged the broken end against the board. She barely had time to look up and take aim before the wooden boar crashed into the makeshift spear. Tam rolled to the side as the board splintered into pieces. Had she done it? Had the weapon struck the right spot?

She didn't bother to get to her feet as they slowed the log, and the judges approached. Tam breathed a sigh of relief when she saw her blade had struck the target. But was it deep enough?

The judges conferred with Steadman for a moment. He nodded. "Four inches! A little non-traditional, but very resourceful. Welcome to round two, number twenty-four."

The audience cheered. Elnor stood, clapping enthusiastically. Her father still stared down at her, his expression unreadable. She tore her gaze away. Willow ran over and helped Tam to her feet, then led her beside the stands as the next competitor was announced. "That was amazing! I admit, even I had some doubts when your weapon broke."

"Yeah, me too, but I had one more pass, so I had to try something. Didn't think it would actually work." Tam sat down cross-legged and leaned against a tree, glad to take her eyes away from the testing even if just for a short time. Tilting her head back, she watched as the leaves blew in the trees overhead. She'd done it and was now one step closer to becoming a Pathfinder.

"Wow, Tam. That was really something," Hendrik said as he approached.

Tam's victory turned bitter in her mouth. She sat up, glaring back at him. "Oh, now you want to act friendly again?"

"What do you mean?"

"You know what I mean. Just stay away from me."

"But I—"

Willow stepped up to Hedrick, her head only coming to his chest. "You heard her. Stay away."

Hendrik ignored her. "I need to get back in case they call my name next, but I just wanted to say congratulations."

"Mmm, well, now you have." Tam leaned back again. A single leaf fell, spinning and turning in a sudden gust until it was out of sight. When she glanced back up, Hendrik was gone.

Willow plopped down next to her. "So, what's the story behind that? Why did you want him to get lost? He's a cute one."

Tam rolled her eyes. "You think they're all cute."

"No, just the cute ones. I don't think Mayor Steadman is attractive at all."

"Oh, balding father figures aren't your type?"

Willow laughed. "Not particularly."

"Okay, well Hendrik isn't my type either. I don't like people who pretend to be your friend to your face and make fun of you behind your back."

"He did that?" Willow furrowed her brow and looked in the direction Hendrik had gone.

"Yeah, he helped me with a few moves yesterday and even gave me some tips. Today, I saw him talking to his friends about me and laughing."

Willow frowned. "Really? That handsome jerk. You want me to rough him up a little?"

Tam shook her head with a laugh. "That's okay. I wouldn't want him to get sent to the medic tent before I have a chance to annihilate him on the next part of the test."

Grinning, Willow nodded. "That's the spirit."

The audience cheered, making the girls turn toward the arena. Another person must have passed.

"Maybe we should get back out there," Tam said.

The mayor's voice boomed as the cheering subsided. "Next up, number twenty, Hendrik Thomson of Sparrow Tribe."

"Well, we can't miss this one," Willow said. "Let's go."

They came back around the stands just in time to see the wooden boar rushing toward Hendrik. Tam sucked in a nervous breath in spite of herself.

Hendrik ran his fingers along the log as it passed until his fingertips could find a handhold. The log drug him for a few seconds before he managed to pull himself up. A little shaky on his feet, he drew back his weapon and brought it down hard. The momentum from the hit was enough to set him off balance. The crowd gasped as he toppled from the log. Hendrik landed awkwardly on his neck, collapsed on himself, and laid unmoving. Tam took several steps forward. A medic was about to run in when Hendrik rolled to the side out of the way of the still swinging log. He got shakily to his feet and gave a reassuring wave. Tam sighed with relief. Even if she didn't like the guy, she didn't want him dead or anything. After all, how would she beat him at the next challenge if he was dead?

The judges ran to the log, brought it to a stop, measured, then remeasured how deep his blade had gone.

"It must be really close," Willow whispered.

Why did Tam feel so nervous? Why should she care if he passed the test? She glanced over at him. He had his eyes squeezed shut and his head down.

Finally, Steadman held up his megaphone. "Three inches!"

Hendrik pumped his fist as the crowd cheered. Breathing hard, he slid down a tree into a sitting position. Grace handed him a cup full of water. As he gulped it down, he caught Tam's eye. She looked away, pretending to scan the crowd. Once again, her dad's face drew her attention.

"Why is my dad here?" Tam wondered aloud. She hadn't expected to see him at the testing grounds today. Not after how angry he'd been. Yet there he was, watching. Was he waiting for her to fail? Waiting to say, "I told you so"? She caught his eye and quickly looked away.

"Your dad is here?" Willow asked, searching the crowd. "Which one is he?"

"He's the serious looking one with the mustache staring this way. I hope he isn't here to try to drag me home." She couldn't think of a more embarrassing prospect than being dragged out of the arena by her dad in front of all these people.

"He can't do that. You passed the first part of the test fair and square."

"You don't know my dad."

But as the test wore on and other trainees took on the boar, he made no attempt to get her. He just watched, his face turning red. Tam wasn't sure if it was from the heat or from anger.

After the first part of the test had ended, only eighteen had successfully taken on the wooden boar. For the others, their Pathfinder journey would either end here, or they'd have to wait to try out again next year.

They were only allowed a few minutes to take a break and get a drink of water before the second part of the test began. The water tasted especially delicious in the heat of the day. Not realizing how thirsty she'd been, she closed her eyes and relished the feeling of the cool water running down her dry throat. Tam didn't know what lay ahead, but knew from watching the test year after year, the first half was easy compared to the second.

Grace and Willow were sitting on a bench talking. Tam wanted to sit to try and control her shaky legs, but she didn't like that Grace girl.

"Over here, Tam," Hendrik called. He patted the empty spot on the bench next to him. With a sigh, Tam walked over and sat down. It would only be a couple minutes. She could handle him for that long.

"You want some smoked pheasant?" He held the food in front of her face.

Tam turned away, trying to seem disgusted, but it smelled great. "No thanks. I'm not hungry." Her stomach growled, betraying her lie. "Well, maybe just a little." She accepted the pheasant and ate the piece in a few short bites. The rich, smoky flavor left her wanting more, but she didn't want to fill up too much when she was still feeling nervous about the next challenge.

Hendrik swallowed his mouthful. "So, why are you mad at me? I thought we were becoming friends."

"I'm not mad." Tam frowned and stared at the leaf on the floor.

"You obviously are."

Balling up her fists, she turned to him. "Okay, fine. Yes, I'm mad. You've been laughing at me all day. First telling your friends about my homemade gear, then whispering with Grace."

"What? I didn't do any of that. Well okay, I listened to Grace, but she was just telling me the technique she planned to use against the boar." He leaned back. "Grace, hey Grace. Tell Tam what we were talking about when you were whispering to me earlier."

Grace tilted her head. "Are you sure you want me to say it out loud? Don't you think it might hurt her feelings?"

"Cut it out, Grace. You know we were talking about fighting technique." He turned back to Tam. "Don't listen to her. She likes to cause trouble."

"Uh huh … And your friends?"

"I was telling them how I fell out of a tree the other day like a clumsy nestling."

Tam raised her brow. "Then why were you all looking at me?"

"Contestants get ready for part two," the mayor boomed.

Hendrik stood, wiping his hands on his pants. "You were standing next to the tree I fell from. Not everything's about you, Tam." He gave an infuriating grin as he walked away.

Chapter Five

Tam stood behind a chalk line as Mayor Steadman described the second part of the test. An obstacle course. She could do this.

"As Pathfinders, you must have incredible stamina," Steadman went on. "This race will not only show who is fastest but will weed out those who lack the stamina to go a considerable distance without rest. A path has been marked off through Falcon territory and beyond. You will be required to run, dodge, climb, and swing. You must complete the round three times. Only half of you will move on."

A gasp rose from the contenders. They had already lost so many.

"Yes, you heard me right. After this challenge, nine of you will not be joining the Pathfinders. This course is incredibly dangerous. One fall could get you seriously injured or killed. We have roped it off below and added nets to places where trainees are most likely to fall. However, we could not net everything off, and there is no guarantee a kapros will not be passing below. Pathfinders will be standing by to assist, but they can't be everywhere at once. Do *not* wait for help. If you fall and are able, get to the trees immediately. But my best advice to you is as follows: Don't fall."

Oh, that was helpful. Tam shifted her feet. She had to win. She'd raced home often enough to do her chores and keep out of trouble while training. Hopefully that would serve her well now. Only half would get through. That just meant she had to cross the finish line in ninth place or above. It seemed doable. Pulling out her climbing equipment, Tam groaned. Still busted. Grabbing a strip of cloth from a rag in her pack, she wrapped the claw tightly. Hopefully the repairs would hold just long enough for her to cross that finish line.

The others were all stretching. Maybe she should be stretching too. Tam raised her knee and pulled on it like the others were doing and almost lost her balance.

Grace giggled beside her and said something to Hendrik and another boy with cropped brown hair. They both laughed, and Tam dropped her gaze. Willow was several rows down in the other direction. The girl jogged in place with the tip of her tongue poking out of the corner of her mouth. Tam wished she'd found a spot next to her, but it was too late now.

"Trainees, get ready," Steadman shouted. "Three …"

Tam saw the others putting one foot out behind them and crouching down. She put her left foot back.

"Two …"

That felt funny. Maybe she should try putting her right foot back.

"One …"

That felt funny too. Maybe she should —

"Go!"

Everyone sped off in a flurry except for Tam. The crowd laughed and pointed.

With her face burning, she sprang forward to catch up and reached the back of the line, but the gap between first and last place was growing. Tam passed two runners, now three. The first part of the course was over uneven pathways. Already out of breath, she stumbled, catching herself on the railing. A boy she'd passed earlier went by, not even breaking a sweat.

"Pace yourself, Tam" she chided herself.

Some narrow spots didn't even have railings. It was amazing no one had fallen over the side. Living this high above the forest floor had a way of teaching good balance. Some hanging nets had been suspended beneath them for a bit of protection, but there were still lots of gaps. Logs swung like pendulums across the path ahead. Tam gasped as a boy ahead of her got struck from the side and fell. To her relief, he landed safely in the net below.

Approaching the pendulums, she slowed. A girl pushed past her and easily went through the logs at full speed. Tam was impressed until the final log caught the girl in the side, and she also went flying into the net below. Tam took a deep breath. This was more about timing than speed. She needed to wait until the first log had just passed. *Right ... now!* The first log narrowly missed her, but she wasn't so lucky with the second. It glanced off her back and spun her around. Her head slammed into the wooden pathway as she went down, just managing to grab the platform as she fell. Lights danced in front of her eyes, and her head throbbed as she hung there. Mustering her strength, she pulled herself back up and lay beneath the swinging pendulum. The wind from the passing log prickled her arms. She waited until she had just felt it pass and jumped to her feet and moved to the next one. Still dizzy, Tam had no time to get her bearing if she hoped to catch up. Seeing her window to get through, she sprang into action, stumbling past the final log and continuing forward.

    She passed a couple people who had paused for a breath at the top of a ladder. Ducking under several clothes lines that stretched all the way across a large gap, she saw the people in first place at the other end of the clothes lines. They were nearing the finish and about to make another round. Tam dashed across a bridge and down a set of stairs, jumping down the last three and landing in a roll before continuing to run. Racing around the corner, she passed another girl. At this rate, she just might make it. Her lungs burned, but she ignored them and tried to keep her breathing steady.

The path ended up ahead. She would have to climb through the trees to continue, but the next tree was out of reach. As she stood pondering how to make the transition, a trainee zipped past her and, using a rope hanging nearby, swung across to the nearest tree and sunk her claws in. How had Tam missed the ropes? There were a couple more hanging between the gap. Tam backed up and ran full speed, leaping from the platform and reaching for a rope. Her fingers stung as they slipped on the rough fibers, but she hung on. She'd have to swing her legs a few times to build enough momentum to reach the tree.

This was the moment of truth. Either her repair to the left claw held, or it didn't. She released the rope on the third swing, sinking her hands and feet into the tree. To her relief, if held just fine. She scaled the tree and leapt to the next and then the next. Tam had to climb around a slow-moving boy, leaping to the final tree, then onto a pathway below. Sprinting the rest of the way, she tried to ignore the muscle fatigue in her arms and legs.

She crossed the line and slowed her pace, only allowing herself twenty seconds, then picking up speed again. *Slow and steady*, she reminded herself. But not *too* slow. The second time around the course went much faster. There were just ten people in front of her. Now she was on the last lap and just had to gain one place. Putting her head down, she gave it everything she had left. Her legs were aching, but there was no letting up now. Tam passed a boy on the bridge and a girl leaning against a tree. She had done it! Tam was in eighth place and back in the game. All she had to do was maintain her speed and not get passed.

Two trainees were ahead of her on the path, vying for seventh place. When they got to a narrow spot, both refused to give an inch and collided. One boy kept his balance and continued, but the other turned his ankle and fell, smacking his side on the wooden path, then rolling off. The crowd gasped. He grabbed a rope just beneath by his fingertips. Tam glanced down. If he fell there, he was going to miss the net by a few feet. She got to the spot where he'd slipped and stretched her hand down, but he was out of reach. Two Pathfinders were making their way over to help, but by the look on the boy's face, he wasn't going to hang on much longer. Without thinking, she jumped to a large branch, then to a platform below. He dangled above her now. Instead of reaching for the boy, she grabbed the net and pulled it as hard as she could, stretching it beneath him and hooking the end over a broken limb. That should catch his fall.

No sooner did she have it in place, the boy's grip gave out, and he screamed. A look of surprise, then relief crossed his face as he bounced harmlessly onto the net. Tam sighed with relief as well, glad that the limb had held, then climbed back up to the walkway as the Pathfinders took over. She started running again but knew it must be too late. Arriving at the spot with the clotheslines, she looked across the way. A big group was about to cross the finish. No way would she make it on time. There was still the climbing portion ahead of her.

Tam looked from the finish and back to the clotheslines. She wouldn't let her dream end here. Not without a fight. Maybe this was smart; maybe it was dumb. In any case, it was completely crazy. Breaking a branch from a nearby tree, she placed it over the downward sloping line with a hand on each side, then took a deep breath, sprinted, and leapt from the platform.

The jolt almost made her lose her grip, but she kept hold, squeezing the branch until her knuckles went white as she zoomed across on her makeshift zipline. Tam was coming in fast. Pulling her legs up, she was preparing to land in a run, when to her horror, the line began to give way.

The rope was falling.

She raised her legs higher, hoping that the momentum would get her to the platform before falling too low. The line swung down, and she landed in a less then graceful roll onto the wooden deck. With no time to ponder just how lucky she'd been, Tam jumped to her feet and plowed through the finish line, collapsing on her hands and knees.

The crowd was silent for a moment while they digested what just happened, then broke out in thunderous applause.

Grace stood above her. "Nice effort for a Sparrow, but you came in 10th place."

Tam held her head in her hands. So close. She'd been so close. Now her dream was over. She'd go back to the cages, continue learning to be a Keeper. Her dad would be happy anyway. She looked up at him, not knowing what to expect. He stared down at her, a thoughtful look on his face. Probably trying to decide what kind of punishment she deserved. When the crowd had died down, Mayor Steadman stepped back up to the podium to announce the names of those who would continue to the next round. Tam moved to a bench, too tired to stand. She didn't really want to stay and hear the rest. She just wanted to go home. As soon as she got her breath back, Tam would slip away.

Steadman read off the names one by one. Each time, the names were met with applause. She recognized a few names. Dover, the strong guy had gotten first place. Hendrik, Grace, and Willow were also part of the nine. Tam glanced up at her new friend and tried to muster up a smile of congratulations.

"That completes the names of those moving to the next round," the mayor said.

Tam stood to go. Time to slip away before the festival started. With any luck, she'd make it back home before her dad and have time to take a nap before the yelling started.

"Also," the man went on, "we would like to take this time to acknowledge number twenty-four, Tam Johansson of Sparrow Tribe."

Tam stopped mid-step and turned around, hunching her shoulders as all eyes snapped to her.

"This individual showed true self-sacrifice when she rescued a competitor and showed ingenuity and courage with that rather unusual finish. These characteristics are what the Pathfinders are all about, and we hope she will try again next year."

The crowd cheered and stomped their feet. "Let her through!" someone yelled. Tam whirled around in shock. That voice. It was_ "Let Tam through," her dad shouted again.

"Yes, let her through," another agreed. Soon, they were all chanting, "Let Tam through. Let Tam through."

Tam's cheeks flushed, and her heart raced. Was that allowed? No, she'd never heard of them letting someone through who failed a test, no matter the circumstances.

Mayor Steadman stepped down from the podium and talked with the judges. General Kaan joined them, a frown on his face. A bead of sweat rolled down Tam's face, and she wiped it away. What was taking them so long? Finally, the circle broke, and the mayor came back, raising his hand for silence.

"The judges and I have conferred with General Kaan, and we have agreed to let Tam join the other trainees in the winner's circle. Please join me in welcoming our tenth member of the Pathfinders!" His announcement was met with thunderous applause.

Tam's breath caught in her throat. Had she heard that right? And her dad of all people shouting for her to get through? What was going on? She caught the General's gaze. His eyes were narrowed as if to say, 'Don't mess this up.'

"We did it!" Willow shouted, giving Tam a big hug and pulling her attention away from his glare. "I knew there was something special about you."

"Yeah, she knows how to cheat," a boy with freckles said.

Hendrik punched him in the arm. "Shut up. Great job, Tam. I knew you could do it." Hendrik grinned so wide, his dimples appeared on both cheeks.

Willow grabbed Tam's arm and led her away from the boys. "Are you okay? You seem a bit shaken up?"

Tam gave herself a shake. "Yeah, yeah I'm fine. Just taking it all in. Just a few minutes ago, I'd resigned myself to being a Keeper for the rest of my life. Now I get another chance? I just need a moment to let it sink in."

Willow smiled. "Well don't take too long. The festivities are about to begin." The festivities. Right, Tam had almost forgotten. Tables and benches were being brought out as they spoke, and a group of musicians had taken the stage. The girls could already hear lyre music and pan whistles blending together in a festive melody as Tam allowed herself to be led to a seat.

Tables laden with fruits, vegetables, nuts, pastries, and all sorts of delicious looking things were wheeled out and lined up near the stands. This was more food than most of the villagers saw all year. But the main attraction was still to come. All eyes turned toward the huge table with a young cooked boar lying on it. It took five men to roll it out. This was a rare treat. Hunting kapros was extremely dangerous and not done often, but it was tradition for the Pathfinders to hunt a boar for the festival each year. One juvenile kapros was so large, it provided plenty of meat for everyone.

Tam kept looking for her father in the crowd, but he was nowhere in sight. It was pretty rare for him to miss the Pathfinder festival. He loved the boar meat so much, he would usually talk about it for weeks leading up to the event.

"Looking for someone?" Willow asked.

"Just my dad. I haven't seen him since … well, since he helped me pass the test. I still don't know why he did that."

"Yeah, I thought you said he was against you becoming a Pathfinder."

"He is. He was. I don't know anymore."

"Maybe when he saw how hardcore you were, he changed his mind."

Tam shrugged. "Maybe. But you don't know my dad. He was so adamant."

"Well, you're on of us now, so relax and worry about your dad later."

Tam nodded. "I'll try. But as she looked around at all the kids who had passed, and thought of the amazing skills they had displayed, butterflies filled her stomach and the seed of doubt grew. How could Tam hope to keep up with these guys if she'd only passed on a technicality?

Chapter Six

Her father wasn't home when Tam returned. It was only after waking up the next morning that she heard him in the kitchen. She'd been listening to the sounds for nearly an hour, trying to will herself out of bed. The thought of confronting her father, even after he stood up for her, filled her with apprehension. The smell of eggs and toast were in the air. Stretching, she swung her legs out of bed and inhaled, allowing the familiar scent to calm her. He wouldn't be making her breakfast if he was really angry, right?

Quickly, she washed up in the basin by her bed, threw on some clothes, and came downstairs. Dad stood at the sink with his back to her. Along with breakfast, a large box sat on the table.

Tam sat down and stared at her father's back. "Good morning."

He grunted in response. Shifting in her chair, Tam searched for something to say to end the awkward silence. "Um ... I didn't see you at the festival. Did you go home?"

"Uh huh," he said without turning around.

Picking at the eggs on her plate, she stared at the box in front of her. It was wooden and dusty with rusted hinges. She was a bit surprised Dad would put something that dirty on the table.

"So … what's in the box?"

Finally, he turned. His eyes looked dark as if he hadn't gotten much sleep. Was he up all night worrying? Tam felt another pang of guilt. "Go ahead, and open it. It's yours."

"Mine?" She didn't remember owning an old box. Leaning forward, she lifted the lid. The hinges creaked as it opened. The contents were covered in burlap. "What is this?"

Her dad cleared his throat. "It's the reason I came home early."

Tam lifted the burlap. Nestled inside was a set of climbing claws, shoe spikes, a shiny shoka, and a gold pin with two crisscrossed grains of wheat. It was the symbol for Sparrow district. "Whca," Tam whispered.

"I was up half the night making sure everything still worked and getting it oiled and shined up."

"But, how? Where did it all come from?"

Dad shifted his footing and met Tam's curious gaze. "They … well, they belonged to your mother."

Tam frowned. Why would Mom have these?

Dad took a deep breath. "Tam, your mother and I were Pathfinders."

"Wait, what?" Tam's vision blurred. The knothole she'd been staring at on the table now resembled a giant blurry beetle. "Why didn't you tell me?"

"Because I didn't want you to try and follow in her footsteps. I didn't want you to throw your life away."

She balled up her fists. "You had no right to keep this from me. I deserved to know the truth."

"You're right. And I meant to tell you eventually."

"When? Were you going to wait until I was too old to be a Pathfinder? Was that your plan?"

"No, I … I didn't have a plan."

"Was she good?" Tam spoke while running her fingertips over the blurry knothole.

"What?"

"Was she a good Pathfinder?"

"The best. Head of our team and the top fighter in our whole unit." His eyes glazed over as he remembered with a smile. "She was dedicated to the needs of the village and very talented.

He picked up the pin from the box and fastened it on Tam's shirt over her heart. Your mother never went anywhere without her pin. She was a proud Sparrow through and through."

Tam touched the pin in awe, staring down at it with pride. "So it's true then? What Gran said. Mom was killed by kapros?"

He nodded. "Yes, it's true."

Tam's head spun, thankful she was already sitting down. "Then why did you tell me she was killed by the earthquake?"

"I said she was killed during the earthquake, not by it." He rubbed his temple. "I think I need some coffee for this conversation." He walked over to the stove and put a kettle on, then turned around, leaning against the counter. "Your mother was ... Well, your mother was helping evacuate part of the village most affected by the earthquake. It should have been a simple job, but a little girl fell to the forest floor when the railing gave way. Her leg was broken. Your mom fought off an entire sounder of kapros while the girl was taken to safety. I was with the rest of our team on the other side of the village rescuing a family whose home was collapsing. By the time we got there ..." He paused, choked with emotion. "By the time we got there, it was too late." He cleared his throat. "I was told she fought 'til she had no breath left in her."

Tam's eyes welled with tears. "You should have told me the truth ...."

"Yes, I should have."

He picked up the pin from the box and fastened it on Tam's shirt over her heart.

Tam wiped away her tears and touched the pin in awe, staring down at it with pride.

Turning back to the box, she lifted a claw and placed it on her hand. The spikes were still hidden inside the glove. She put it against the crate, and the spikes immediately sprung out, sticking into the wood. "Pressure sensitive? These are amazing! But why are you giving them to me? I thought you didn't want me to be a Pathfinder."

"I didn't. I mean, I don't." He sat down across from her, rubbing the stubble on his chin.

"Then, why?"

"Because," he said with a sigh. "Yesterday, I was furious. I was ready to ground you for the foreseeable future. Keep you on a rope if I had to until I could get some sense into that thick skull of yours. But then …"

"Then?"

"Then I saw you out there. I saw how you put your future on the line to rescue that boy without a second thought. I saw how you took a chance with that clothesline, which was very foolish I might add, but also incredibly brave. As I watched, I realized you …" His voice shook with emotion. Hastily, he wiped a tear away. "You reminded me of her. You reminded me of your mother."

"Dad, I—"

"Let me finish. Your mother may have lost her life that day, but she saved many others. You were right. Aviary needs people like you and your mother. For me to keep you here when you have that potential running through your veins would be like keeping the cure for a horrible disease buried in the ground because I'm afraid it might get lost."

Tam swallowed. A cure? Aviary needed people like her? A knot formed in her stomach. She was glad Dad was being encouraging, but living up to her mom's reputation was a huge pressure. "I don't know, Dad. There are a lot of people out there stronger than I am."

"Maybe stronger here," he said, pointing to her arm. "But not here." As he spoke, he put his hand over her heart, covering the Sparrow pin. He gave her a rough embrace. She buried her face in her shoulder, inhaling the scent of pine and coffee grounds. Her mom, a Pathfinder? This explained so much, yet she was having a hard time wrapping her mind around it. If her mom was the best, and even *she* had been killed by the kapros, what chance did Tam have?

Her dad stepped back. When he spoke, his voice was husky. "You better get a move on. I don't want you to be late for your first day of training."

"Oh, right." She'd nearly forgotten. "I'll just run out and make sure the birds have fresh seed and water."

"No. I won't have you be late on your first day. I'll take care of it this time. I packed a bag with some of your things since you'll be staying at the Pathfinder base now." He set a satchel on the table in front of her. "You can come back and get more of what you need later."

Tam nodded. "Yes, sir." She gulped down an egg and started stuffing the climbing gear in her bag. Going out, she stopped with her hand on the door. "Thanks, Dad. I'll come home every chance I get."

He grunted and waved her on. "Hurry up now, or you'll be late."

Slinging the bag over her shoulder, Tam made her way to the Pathfinder base. She couldn't believe Dad was okay with this now, and that he and her mother had been Pathfinders. It was too crazy for her to even process. Tam would have to do well to live up to his confidence in her. All the other trainees had been training much longer than her. Would they kick her out if she couldn't keep up? No, she couldn't think like that. Somehow, she'd find a way, and she couldn't wait to try out her new gear.

Tam had never been allowed through the gates leading to the base before. Pathfinders were supposed to train with no distractions, so they mainly kept to themselves. How would they know to let her in now?

As she walked along, footsteps thudded behind her. Glancing over her shoulder Tam saw the strong guy from yesterday. "Dover, right?" she asked as he came up alongside.

He nodded. "And you're … Pam?"

"Close. Tam," she said with a smile.

"Sorry. I'm not very good with names." Dover wore a plain brown t-shirt. His muscles bulged under the fabric. He looked her up and down. "Cool Sparrow pin."

"Oh … uh, thanks. And don't worry. I'm not usually good with names either, but you were memorable."

"I was? Why is that?"

Tam's cheeks flushed. "Erm, you were the only one to practically decapitate that log."

"Oh." Dover's eyes sparkled. "Well, I remember you too. Not everyone finishes the obstacle course with such style."

"Ha, thanks but I almost fell." Tam slowed her steps as the wooden gate came into view. "How are we supposed to get in?"

"Oh, they gave me a password." Dover held up a small piece of folded paper. "Didn't you get one?"

"No, but I left a little early last night."

They had come to a tall wooden gate between two giant redwoods. Dover pounded on the door with his fist. A man appeared above them. "Ah, the new little fledglings in training. You're late. Do you remember the password? I've been instructed not to let you in if you can't follow your first simple direction."

Tam let out a breath, glad she'd run into Dover. How embarrassing if her journey to become a Pathfinder ended because of a password.

Dover opened his mouth to speak, but the man held up a hand. "Wait, don't tell me yet. I'm coming down. You need to each tell me individually. You, boy, back away from the gate so the little lady can go first. I'll watch until you've gone, then come down."

Panic bubbled up in Tam's throat as Dover stepped back. She searched his face, looking for any clue to the password. He widened his eyes and kept glancing down. Did he mean the deck? His shoes? She couldn't be sure. Finally, he put a hand to his satchel and gave it a shake. Before turning and disappearing around the trees.

"Okay. I'll be right there," the man said. His footsteps echoed on the hard wood as he climbed down the steps.

She closed her eyes. Was the password bag or satchel? Maybe tote or pack? Could he have been referring to the color of his bag? It had been a dark, chestnut brown. There were still too many variables, and she was almost out of time. Maybe the password had something to do with the gear in the bag. Tam flipped it open, hoping to gain inspiration when something white caught her eye. It was a small scrap of folder paper. Good old Dover! He must have slipped it into her bag before he left. She would certainly owe him one. A window in the gate opened just as Tam finished smoothing it out.

"Tiger paw," she read aloud.

"Very good. Come on in," he said, slamming the little window. The doors swung open immediately, and Tam stepped inside. The man held out his hand in greeting. "I'm Smitty."

Tam took his hand in hers. "Hi, I'm —"

"Tamerelda. Yes, I know."

"Tam," she corrected.

"Well, Tam, I've been instructed to tell you to meet with the other fledglings in section two which is just beyond the wall and to the left. Off you go." Right as he finished speaking, he whirled around and yelled, "Next!" through the open gate, making Tam jump.

"Thanks," she murmured and turned to go. She couldn't believe she was finally here. The large platform had a huge tree through the center with a walkway carved through it and shops on each side with some of the latest climbing gear and weapons in the window. It was like a little town hidden away within Aviary. Tam paused to look at some fresh bread on a cart. Her mouth watered at the smell. Did they bake it here or have it delivered from one of the bakers in the colony?

"Two small loaves please," Dover said from behind her. A woman in an apron appeared behind the cart and took the coins from Dover's outstretched hand.

"Thanks," Tam said as he handed her one of the loaves.

"Sure. We've got to keep up our strength, right?"

Tam nodded, and they started walking toward the tree in the center. She glanced at his biceps. "Yes, some of us more than others. And thank you for helping me get past the gate. That would have been awful to get sent home the first day."

Dover seemed distracted as they went through the opening. "No problem. That man ... Smithy?"

"Smitty."

"Right. See? I am bad with names. Anyway, Smitty said something about a wall. Do you see a wall?"

"There." She pointed to some people climbing in the distance. As they approached the wall, she leaned her head back, trying to see the top, but it disappeared into the canopy above. They stopped for a moment and watched the climbers jumping from one handhold to another. Tam was alarmed to see they didn't have any safety ropes in place.

The climbers were incredible and fast. Two of them were competing, grabbing brightly colored flags that were placed in various spots on the wall. Finally, one dinged a bell and began making his way back down. The other person, a woman just a few years older than Tam, rang the bell a few seconds later.

"Ha, beat your record, Cassia!" the man said as he dropped to the ground.

Cassia dropped down to join him and grinned. "Oh really? She pointed to a single blue flag above. Missing something?"

The man frowned. "I could have sworn I got them all."

"No swearing in front of the fledglings, Jones." Cassia winked at them. "Shouldn't you be at your first training session?"

Tam's face flushed. "We're heading there now."

"Well, I'll come with you. I'm heading that way too. Keep at it, Jones. You'll get it."

Jones turned purple. "Rematch, right now."

"Later. Gotta get these fledglings to section two." She waved to Tam and Dover, indicating they should follow, and started walking. She kept a brisk pace. Tam had to trot to keep up.

"I saw you both at the test last night. Very impressive."

Dover smiled. "Thanks. You were pretty incredible yourself just now."

"That? Oh, well Jones and I have a long-standing rivalry on that wall. He's getting closer to beating me than I'd like to admit."

As they came around the corner, Tam saw Willow, Hendrick, Grace, and the other fledglings standing in a line ahead.

"You guys are late," Grace commented. "Lucky for you, so is our instructor. I guess the higher ranks can't be bothered with us lowly fledglings. Probably washing their hair."

Cassia stepped from behind Dover. "Well I couldn't very well show up with dirty hair, could I?"

Grace's eyes bulged. "Oh, I, um …"

Tam grinned at her discomfort and joined the others in line. Two more Pathfinders soon appeared and stood next to Cassia.

Cassia inclined her head toward the two men. "These are your other commanders, Yohan and Dorn." Yohan had jet black hair and a dark complexion. Dorn had almond shaped eyes, large muscles, and close-cropped blond hair with a short beard to match.

"Now, let's get started. First, I need to separate you into three groups. A, B, and C." As she spoke, Cassia drew invisible lines between them. Tam was placed with Dover, Hendrick, and Willow. Even though she had to be in a group with Hendrick, at least Grace was on squad B. "Squad A, you're with me. Squad B you're with Yohan, and squad C will be with Dorn."

"Because of the rather unusual exception in Tam's case," Cassia went on, "there will be four members in squad A instead of three."

"Cheater," one of Grace's team members said while pretending to cough into his hand. Grace smiled and gave him a high five.

Cassia glared at him. "Something to say, James?"

"Just a little tickle in my throat."

"Then get some water, and keep your mouth shut."

Tam was really starting to like Commander Cassia.

James lowered his head and shuffled his feet. "Yes, ma'am. Sorry, ma'am."

"Now, get a good look at your teammates. Hopefully, you can stand looking at those mugs because starting today they are your official squad members." As she spoke, she paced in front of them. "Whether you like it or not, you're going to be seeing a lot of each other. As members of the same squad, you hold your teammate's lives in your hands. Additionally, if one of your members does something foolish, you will all be held responsible. You are one unit. Understand?"

They nodded.

"I said, do you understand?" she asked again. "Speak up."

"Yes, ma'am!" they all echoed.

"Very good. Now B and C, follow your commanders. Squad A, come with me."

They followed Cassia down a bridge to an archery range. Several people were practicing on targets made of haybales and wooden planks. She stopped them under a canopy. Bows were lined up in front of them on a table. Cassia walked to the table and faced them.

"Now, who can tell me the most vulnerable spots on a kapros?" she asked.

"Heart, lungs, and spinal cord," Willow answered.

"Yes, and what are the best ways to hit these vital places?"

Willow raised her hand again.

"Let's let someone else answer this one. Tam?"

Tam looked up, trying to recall what she'd learned from the test the day before. "Oh, um … a shoka chop to either the back of the neck or a stab from under the left or right arm."

"Very good. Though keep in mind, the males build up such a thick armor on their neck and shoulders, chopping through it is next to impossible. Now, where do you think arrows might come in handy? Hendrik?"

Hendrik shrugged. "I'm not sure."

"Well, you all forgot to mention one other vital spot. The brain," Smitty said, tapping his forehead.

Dover frowned. "But isn't the skull too thick to penetrate?"

"Yes, however," Cassia said, "we've recently discovered a new way to kill kapros by shooting the creature directly in the eye and piercing the brain. The eye is small and is not an easy target. This should not be attempted unless the archer has a clear shot. If you take the shot and miss, getting an arrow stuck in another area, it will kick up into a frenzy and become far more aggressive and dangerous, possibly even knocking down trees. And if you wound a young one, it will let out a terrible squeal, and if there are any other kapros nearby, they may be drawn to that sound and then you'll have an even more serious problem. Now, as you know, kapros cannot look up." As she spoke, she handed a bow to each of them. "This is both an advantage and disadvantage when it comes to fighting them. Because of the angle of their eyes and brain, you must hit them straight on from the eye level of the pig. Since a long, clear shot is rare in the forest, it forces the shooter to practically go head to head against an often-charging animal."

Tam's hands shook, remembering her close encounter with the kapros on the forest floor. She wiped the sweat from her brow and stepped up to the table. Arrows were laid out in front of them.

"Since this is a relatively new technique, I don't expect you to be experts. I know most of you have some experience with the bow, but for boar hunting, you must be extremely accurate. I trust you will improve quickly with plenty of practice. Now, take your places."

Finally, something where Tam might be able to keep up with the others. Most of them had learned bow skills for bird hunting growing up, but nothing too serious. If they hadn't really been trained on the bow either, maybe she stood a chance of not making a fool out of herself.

After showing them the proper way to stand and hold the bow, Cassia stepped back. "Alright, let's see what you got. Release when ready."

Tam held the bow in front of her with an arrow nocked in the string. She pulled it back, testing the weight. It was a heavier draw weight than the one she used as a kid. Dover didn't hesitate and effortlessly pulled the string back, took aim, and fired. The arrow whizzed through the air, striking the target just a little to the left of the bullseye.

He frowned. "Missed it."

As he went for another arrow, Tam drew back her bow again. The tension made her arm wobble. Taking a deep breath, she let it fly. The string snapped forward with a twang. She winced as the sting slapped her arm, leaving behind a welt. The arrow didn't even make it to the target. Grimacing and putting her hand to her face, Tam peeked through her fingers. Luckily everyone seemed busy with their own shots. Nocking another arrow, she drew it back again, this time keeping her arm slightly bent to avoid the string hitting it again. Pulling it back with all her might, Tam let it go. It shot harder this time, but the arrow went up, high into the air and back down. There was a smaller bow on the table beside them. Maybe she would give that one a try.

"That draw weight is way too heavy for you," Hendrik commented as she was setting it down.

Tam stopped with her hand still on the bow.

"You should try a smaller one," he suggested.

Narrowing her eyes, Tam lifted the bow again and nocked another arrow. She wasn't going to give him the satisfaction. Raising the bow, she planted her feet like Cassia had shown her. Drawing back the string in one fluid motion, she took careful aim at the red circle in the center of the target and released it. The arrow flew, straight and even. Tam held her breath. When the arrow struck, she was elated. She'd hit the target!

"Ha! Too heavy, eh?" Tam grinned with satisfaction.

"Much better," Cassia said. "But next time, try and hit your own target."

"Oh, oops." Tam let out a nervous laugh. Her arrow had hit the target to the left.

"You might want to try a lighter draw weight as Hendrik suggested. Just until you build strength in that arm."

Tam smiled weakly. "Yeah, maybe."

But she didn't. Stubbornly, Tam kept the same bow all afternoon and felt she'd shown some real improvement. About 80% of her arrows still missed, but that 20% gave her hope. By the time they took a break, her muscles were aching and burning, and her arm throbbed from where the string had grazed several more times. After they'd had a few moments to rest and have a snack, Cassia made them run laps around the edges of the camp to build endurance. Tam was thankful climbing wasn't on the list of activities for the day. The way her arm felt, she didn't think she could hold up a potato let alone her own weight.

By the end of the day, she was exhausted. A girl just a year or two older than Tam arrived and showed them to where they would be staying so they could wash up before dinner. The first years and second years stayed in the same barracks with separate rooms for men and women. There was a weapon room that doubled as a small dining area and kitchen adjoining the two rooms, but tonight, they were expected to eat outside with those from other barracks.

Tam rinsed off in the shower made from a large tin can with holes poked in it, then changed into fresh clothes. She looked over the schedule Cassia had given her as she walked out the door and into the weapon room. When Tam joined the Pathfinders, she imagined her training would consist of fighting and learning climbing techniques, but each day, they were also expected to attend other classes. Most of the classes were about survival. Tomorrow, they would learn about what plants and fruits were safe to eat, and later, they would learn how to construct a temporary dwelling in the trees.

"What did you guys do today?"

Tam turned to see Grace sitting at one of the tables. "Oh, uh, we mostly did archery."

"Not you. I was talking to him," she said, pointing to Hendrik who sat at the table just beyond where Tam stood.

Tam's cheeks burned. How was she supposed to know where the other girl was looking?

"What did you guys do today, Hendrik?" she asked again, this time emphasizing his name.

"Like Tam said, we did archery. You really should work on your listening skills."

Ignoring his comment, Grace hopped down from the table and sat so close to Hendrik, he had to lean back to keep their faces from being inches apart.

She smiled. "Tell me all about it. I'll bet you were the best one."

Rolling her eyes, Tam left the room. She'd hardly eaten all day, and now her stomach kept loudly reminding her.

Spotting Dover and Willow around the big slab fire pit, Tam went to join them. Everyone was roasting potatoes, carrots, and quail over the fire. Grabbing a stick, she shoved some food on the end and sat down next to Willow. Watching the fire flicker and pop, she thought about her mother's first day here. Had it been similar? The thought made her feel happy, connected. She knew so little about her, and this new information still made her head spin. Was her mom this sore? Probably not if she'd trained for years beforehand like the others. How long had Tam been training? Six months? That sneaking bit of doubt welled up inside her again. How was she going to keep up with everyone after being this tired the first day?"

"Hey, Tam. Didn't you hear me?" Willow asked.

"Huh?"

"I said your food is on fire."

"Oh, oops." Tam brought the stick closer and blew on the flames until they went out. The quail was burnt beyond recognition.

"You want another piece?" Dover asked.

"Oh, no. It's okay. I like it crispy."

"You seemed a million miles away just then. Come to think of it, you've been a bit distracted all day. What have you been thinking about?" Willow asked.

"I've just been thinking about something my dad told me before I left."

"Oh? Do you want to talk about it?"

Tam considered for a moment. Was she ready to talk about her mom yet? What would they think? Would they have unrealistic expectations if they knew? She shook her head. If she didn't talk to someone about this, her chest might burst. Maybe speaking it aloud would help her grasp it more fully. Making up her mind, Tam cleared her throat.

"It turns out, my dad's been lying to me for years." She glanced around to make sure no one was listening. Dover and Willow leaned closer, intrigued.

"My mom and dad were both Pathfinders, and my mom didn't die from the earthquake like he led me to believe. She died while trying to save a girl from the kapros. She held an entire sounder off on her own until the girl was safe."

"Woah ... That's amazing," Willow said.

Dover tilted his head like a curious dog. "What was your mom's name? I'm pretty familiar with all the Pathfinder families."

"Her name was Renli Johansson."

Willow tilted her head, mouthing the name. "Seems familiar." Her mouth dropped open. "Wait a minute. Your mom was Ren?"

"Yeah, that was my dad's pet name for her. Why? Have you guys heard of her?"

Dover nodded vigorously. "She is a legend among Pathfinders. Everyone's heard of Ren."

"Really?"

"Well, yeah. Ren was the best of the best. She came up with a lot of the Pathfinder methods they still use today."

"And you're her daughter?" Willow grinned. "I knew you were special."

Tam swallowed. What had she done? No way could she live up to that with her stick arms and weak muscles.

"Your mom was Ren?"

Tam turned. Grace stood behind her, arms folded. "Oh man. That's rich! Hey everyone, this scrawny kid is Ren's daughter."

Everyone around her began to murmur in surprise. Some looked at her with eyes raised, while others scoffed and shook their heads. "Guess the apple *did* fall far from the tree in your case. You're not even the same kind of fruit. Just a shriveled grape. Maybe Ren wasn't as great as they say. Maybe she was a cheat too."

Tam stood up, fists clenched.

Dover stood up too and stepped between them. "Hey now. Let's not fight on our first night here. It's time to celebrate. We're all on the same team, remember?" He narrowed his eyes in Grace's direction. "I think you owe Tam an apology."

Grace held up her hands. "You are so right. I'm sorry, Tam. You aren't a lowdown cheat that belongs on the farm digging holes." She gave Dover an angelic smile, then cast a scornful scowl in Tam's direction. But Dover didn't seem to notice.

"There, that's more like it," he said, sitting back down.

Still fuming, Tam sat back down and took an angry bite of her quail. "Ow," she said as her teeth clamped down on the hard blackened meat. She set it aside with a sigh. "I know I shouldn't let her get to me, but I think … I think part of me worries Grace might be right." Tam had said too much, and now her eyes were beginning to well up with tears. *Great, now everyone really will think I'm a powder down.* She tried to hide her watery eyes by pretending to yawn and failed. Her fake yawns always looked awkward. Like she was singing a silent opera.

"None of that," Dover said. "We both saw you at the Pathfinder test. You were awesome! Right, Willow?"

"Yes, totally. Don't let her get to you."

Just then Hendrik came outside and plopped down across from them. "Hey, guys." He looked from Tam's red eyes and back to the other two. "Are you okay, Tam? What happed? Did I miss something?"

Tam waved away his questions. "No. I … The smoke is getting in my eyes."

"Right," Willow agreed. "It *is* pretty smokey."

Tam gave a nod of silent thanks in the other girl's direction, grateful for the backup. Hendrik scratched his head as he looked at the clean burning wood, then shrugged.

"Okay. Well, did you guys hear about the mission in a couple weeks?"

Tam, glad for the change of subject, raised her eyebrows. "What mission?"

"In just two weeks' time, we'll be sent out on our very first mission," Dover chimed in. He held two sticks over the fire, laden with only quail.

"What? Already?" Tam removed the burnt quail from her roasting stick, loaded it up with potatoes and held it over the fire, her mouth watering from all the smells.

"Yes," Willow said, nodding enthusiastically. "Isn't is exciting? We don't know what the mission will be yet, but it will probably require us to stay out in the wild overnight."

"Will Cassia be with us?" Tam asked. "Of course, she must be going."

"No, that's the most exciting part. We'll be completely on our own."

"But they haven't even taught us how to use grapplers yet. Will they give them to us before the mission?" Grapplers were the grappling guns that fastened at the waist and allowed Pathfinders to shoot through the trees at a sometimes dangerously fast rate.

Willow shook her head. "No, we won't get to train with those until after the mission. They're part of the reward for completing it."

Tam swallowed. "I just hope we're ready."

Chapter Seven

The following days were filled with learning things like what to do if they fell on the forest floor, how to sneak above a boar undetected, and lessons in first aid. They did a little archery each day, along with shoka practice and climbing. Each night, Tam went to bed sore and tired but happy knowing she was making progress.

Today, her first class was another first aid lesson. Tam opened her eyes and sat up. The room was empty.

"Ah man," Tam said with a sigh, realizing she must have slept in. She swung her legs out of bed, dressed, and quickly ran her fingers through her hair, pulling it back in a ponytail. Grabbing some berries on the way out the door, Tam made her way to sector two, which was where most of their classes were held.

As she sprinted to make up for lost time, a shape came out of the doorway to her left. Not able to stop herself in time, she crashed into the figure and rolled to the floor.

"Hey, what's the big idea?!" Grace yelled. Standing and turning toward the offending person. Her frown deepened when she saw Tam sprawled out next to her.

"Sorry," Tam said with a sheepish grin.

"Of course it's you."

"Well, good morning to you, too," Tam muttered, wiping the pine needles from her shirt. "Why aren't you in class already? You're usually early."

"Not that it's any of your business, but I needed get some new gear."

"New gear? Don't you already have really nice gear?"

"The standard stuff is all fine and well for the average Pathfinder, but my family are Falcons and are expert Craftsman. We've always used state of the art modifications. I just had hydraulic powered razor spikes installed in my gloves. They insert into the trees with ease and cut in like butter. Plus, they have a quick release feature. No more having to yank my hands free with unnecessary energy I could use for climbing." She leaned closer. "Plus, I just got my first grappler, and it launches further and with more accuracy than the wimpy ones they're going to hand out at the end of the first mission."

Tam's eyes went wide. "That's amazing, but … is that allowed? Aren't we supposed to wait to use those?"

Grace glared at the other girl. "My family have been Pathfinders for generations unlike your hick farmer family. We know what's best for us. And if you know what's best for you, you'll keep quiet."

Tam shrugged. "Do what you want. I don't care."

"Grace!" a boy called from across the way. "Come on. We're late."

Without another word, Grace turned and ran, leaving Tam standing by the shop. She gave a start, remembering she was running late too, and dashed off. When she arrived at the outdoor classroom, her squad was listening intently as Cassia pointed to a picture of a skeleton and demonstrated proper wrapping technique. The instructor became silent as Tam approached.

"Sorry. I'm so sorry," Tam said. Her cheeks flushing.

"Don't make this a regular thing, Miss Johansson."

"I won't."

"Many of the others have gone through these things in training before the Pathfinder test. As you are aware, your circumstances are unique, and you need every opportunity to catch up and improve."

Tam's face grew even hotter. "Yes, ma'am," she mumbled.

"What was that?"

"Yes, ma'am," Tam repeated, louder this time.

"Good. Now you'll be paired with Hendrik. You'll be field dressing a broken left leg to ensure it stays immobile during a return from the wilds to base. Hopefully you've been studying the manual since you missed most of the lesson."

Tam swallowed. She hadn't read all of the section on first aid yet, but how hard could it be?

Grabbing a roll of gauze, Tam set to work. Several moments later, she stepped back to admire her work.

"Ouch!" Hendrik said, flexing his legs and wiggling his toes. Tam had completely wrapped Hendrik legs together with white gauze and had wrapped the material part way up his torso.

Stepping forward, she wrapped another strip around his stomach. "Stay still. It won't hurt if you stop squirming."

"Are you sure this is how you treat a broken leg? Why do you need to wrap it that high?"

Pausing, Tam sat back on her heels to examine her work. "Of course. You've got to keep your leg aligned with the rest of your body, or it will heal crooked... I think." She scratched her head, glancing around at the other fledgling's work. Willow had a small but neat wrap around a splint on Dover's leg. "That should do it!"

"Hmm ... I may have overdone it," Tam said with a frown.

Hedrick smirked. "You think?"

Cassia walked between the recruits, either giving nods of approval or offering direction. "Very nice work, Willow."

The girl beamed. "Thanks!"

"Too bad you fixed the wrong leg. It was supposed to be the left one, not the right."

Willow's cheeks flushed. "Oh."

"And Tam ..." Cassia looked Hendrik up and down. "A little excessive don't you think?"

Tam gave a weak smile. "Well at least I got the left leg."

"Yes, and the right, and the torso." Cassia turned to face the others. "Never forget that in the wilds, supplies are limited, and we must ration everything, even our medical supplies."

Tam nodded. "Sorry," she mumbled. "I'll do it over."

Cassia grunted. "No time. We'll go over it again later. Right now, we need to meet with the other squads for a special stealth drill before lunch."

Tam's stomach growled at the mention of food. Lunch couldn't come soon enough. She'd been in such a hurry that morning, she hadn't eaten anything.

"A little help here?" Hendrik called.

"Oh, right." She bent down and tried to loosen the knots secured around his body. "What have you heard about a stealth drill?" she asked.

He shrugged. "Not much."

"I've heard they have you sneak up behind ravens while they are eating and attempt to claim a ribbon from around their foot without them taking off," Dover chimed in. "At least that's what they did when my cousin did it a few years ago."

"Wow, that sounds difficult," Tam said with a frown.

"Enough chit chat," Cassia called from across the platform. "We need to meet up with the others in sector five."

Willow gasped.

"What is it?" Tam asked her.

"Don't you remember what they said about sector five at orientation?"

Tam shook her head. It was all kind of a blur.

Licking her lips, Willow babbled on excitedly. "They said sector five was off limits. Now we'll finally get to see why. It's so secret that it's not even part of Aviary. You have to ride a huge zipline to get to it."

Tam's heart thudded as they made their way to sector five. Why did she suddenly feel afraid? She'd grown up handling various birds and ravens her whole life. There was nothing scary about trying to take a ribbon from their leg. Difficult, yes. Scary, no way. Yet, as they climbed the ladder leading to the upper story, her chest was heavy with dread.

Chapter Eight

Their team was the last to reach the top. The two other squads were already there. One by one, they were being harnessed to a large zip line, face down, then sent flying headfirst at a rapid speed. They were higher up now than she had ever been. Tam looked down and instantly felt dizzy. She stood behind Willow to wait her turn, her heart thumping. Was it excitement? Fear? Probably a little of both.

Willow was tied into the harness now. With a huge grin, she dove off the platform, arms outstretched like a bird. Tam tried to regulate her breathing, then stepped forward. As they secured her to the line, Willow disappear among the trees.

"Alright, you're all set," the man said, giving a final tug on the rope. "Time to fly, little fledgling."

Tam hesitated, and the man gave her a push. Her stomach leapt into her throat as she dropped straight down. Was something wrong? It felt like she was in a free fall. The ropes must not have been tied properly. Tam screamed just as the harness finally caught her and propelled her down the line at high speed.

She gasped as the wind whipped her face, blowing her hair out behind her. The breeze gave her whole body goosebumps, and she struggled to regain her breath. Her nostrils flared, and her lungs were filled with the fresh scent of the forest. Greens and browns zipped passed her in a blur. This was almost like the zip line Tam built herself, except much faster. Closing her eyes, she tried to enjoy the ride. But wait, how was she supposed to stop? Her eyes snapped open just in time to see the trees ahead rapidly approaching. She was going to crash right into them! Tam braced herself for impact and put her hands in front of her face. At the last minute, she felt herself rising and peeked between her fingers. The speed had slowed as she gently glided to the platform where the others were waiting to catch her.

"Quite a rush, eh?" Hendrik said with a wink. "I thought for a minute I was going to crash into the trees."

Tam stood on shaky legs. "No sweat. I wasn't ... I wasn't too worried." She walked over and joined the others at the edge. Her heart was still beating like crazy as she cast a glance down. There were no birds in sight. In front of the platform where they stood, an area of the forest had been sectioned off by an enormous twenty-foot fence that spanned several hundred feet across. The rectangle of land had various trees and rocks with a stream running through the center. At the far end, a huge, brown boulder came to about the center, dominating the landscape.

A tree near the boulder was strung with three ribbons. Blue, red and yellow.

Grace craned her neck to the trees. "Where are the birds? I heard there were going to be birds."

"That was last year," Cassia replied. "We're trying something new this time. We realized we needed to simulate what it will actually be like out there to give you a better sense of the stakes and what you're going to be up against."

Tam swallowed. She didn't like the sound of that.

"Bring it on," Dover said, setting his jaw with determination. "We can handle it."

"Great to hear," Cassia said with a nod. Cassia held her arms up to gain their attention. "Today we will be working on one of the most important aspects of being a Pathfinder. Can anyone guess what it is?"

"Slashing technique!" Dover said.

"No, it's obviously climbing." Grace crossed her arms and cocked an eyebrow at the instructor as if daring her to counter.

Cassia shook her head. "While both of those elements are important, there is one that is even more crucial to survival, and that is-"

"Stealth," Willow chirped in.

"That is correct. Good job, fledgling."

Grace shot a glare at Willow, but Willow didn't seem to notice the daggers being thrown her way.

"A direct confrontation with a kapros is always the last resort. This is why stealth is so important. You will all be working to retrieve your team's flag from that small tree."

Grace frowned. "Okay. So what's the catch?"

Cassia nodded toward the forest floor. "You see that brown thing?"

Squinting, Grace placed her hand over her eyes. "You mean that big boulder?"

"That's no boulder." Cassia took a deep breath, then rang a bell that hung from a branch.

The boulder quivered and shook, as if coming to life. Tam took an involuntary step back, her mind reeling. They wouldn't ... They couldn't ... but they did. Turning toward them, nostrils flaring, stood a large, angry kapros. Its fur bristled as it charged across the field, striking the tree where they stood and making the platform shake.

"What? Are you guys crazy?" James asked, his eyes wide with fear.

Dover, on the other hand, seemed elated. "A real kapros? We get to fight a real kapros? This is amazing! I can take it down. No problem."

"Are you joking?" James argued. "That thing is huge."

Everyone started talking at once, bombarding the instructors with questions.

Cassia held up her hands to silence them. "No one will be fighting anything today. This is a stealth exercise. You are nowhere near ready to take on a live kapros."

Dover's face fell at the news.

"And take note, this is only a baby kapros," Cassia went on.

"A baby?" someone murmured. "But it's so big!"

Cassia held up her hands again to hold back the flurry of questions. "Yes, a baby. A full grown kapros can be two to three times this size. But be under no illusion; although this is only a baby, and its tusks haven't grown in yet, you will still be in very real danger. However, if you follow my instructions carefully and do not face the animal directly, we should have no deaths today."

A few of the fledglings began to laugh but stopped short when they realized she wasn't joking.

"Just as in the wilds, avoidance is key, and one misstep can easily be your last."

A moment of silence followed Cassia's statement, until the silence was broken by the boar ramming the tree again.

"You feel that?"

They nodded.

"A group of full grown kapros would have no trouble taking a tree this small down, and they seldom hunt alone. Once you are spotted, you will have no choice but to flee, or make it to a tree large enough they can't bring down."

"What about fighting?" Dover asked.

"Fighting is always a last resort. Don't forget that." Cassia clapped her hands together. "Now, as you know, these animals have an excellent sense of smell, hearing, and vision. Which means your best bet is to what?"

Willow's hand shot up.

"Yes, Willow?"

"Keep upwind, move quietly, and try to stay high since they can't raise their necks."

Cassia nodded in approval. "Very good."

Tam glanced down at the boar. It had grown tired of ramming the tree and was running back and forth beneath them.

"Your goal today will be to get your team's flag and return here as quickly as possible without alerting the kapros to your presence. As you may have noticed, there are no trees near the flag post. You will have to improvise and not rely on the safety of the treetops to retrieve it. In the wilds, you may not always have the luxury of taking the high ground."

Tam scanned the surroundings, realizing for the first time how few trees there were. Shivering, she rubbed her arms, remembering her last encounter. These guys were fast. Fast and brutal. Even with her friends help, how would they make it to the flag before it was on top of them? The kapros had finally settled down. It walked back to a pile of leaves and sat with its back to the group, occasionally sniffing the air.

Grace puffed out her chest. "No problem. We're ready." She turned to consult the others on her squad, but Cassia shook her head.

"Today you won't be competing with your squad. The teams will be random. You need to learn to adjust and work with all members of the unit. Not just those you're used to."

Tam's face fell. She may not like Hendrik much, but at least she was used to him and the others. They knew each other's strengths and weaknesses. Working with the others was going to be much more challenging.

Cassia pointed to Hendrik. "Count off by threes starting with you."

As they went along the row, Tam shifted her feet, staring down at the planks below. What if she made a fool of herself in front of everyone? Aware of the sudden silence, she glanced up to see everyone looking at her expectantly.

Her cheeks warmed. "Oh, uh, sorry." Tam hazarded a guess at her number. "Um ... three?" The guess must have been correct, because they continued counting down the row until everyone had sounded off.

"Alright, all ones here," Cassia said, pointing to her far left, "twos here, and threes to my right." Tam moved toward the other threes and wrinkled her nose.

Grace spotted her walking her way and stiffened. "Great. Our team is already at a huge disadvantage."

Tam ignored her and stood on the other side, trying her best to look bored with the whole situation. Her palms were already sweating, and her hands shook, but she was determined to show them all she had earned her spot here just like the rest. She would live up to her mother's legacy and make her proud.

"Hey, listen up. I don't want us to lose because you've got your head in the clouds," Grace said with a sneer.

Tam snapped back to attention. Cassia was explaining the drill. She held up several strips of cloth. "The flags you are trying to collect will look like this. They are all located near the big tree near the center of the arena. Often objects like food, water, and even our own fallen friends must be retrieved from the ground below, and we never know when there might be a stray kapros nearby. You've already had classes on shadow, movement, and camouflage. Now is the time to put those skills to the test. Speed is of the essence, and the best time wins. If anyone on your team is seen by the kapros, your team will be docked five minutes. Stay hidden as much as possible and do *not* engage. The losers from each team will clean the latrines tonight, and the winners will get an extra serving of dessert. Good luck, fledglings."

After Cassia answered a couple more questions, she allowed them a few moments to discuss their strategy. There were four people on Tam's team, and the only one she really knew was Grace. The other two were Creed, a stocky boy, and

Nick, who looked like he would be good at sneaking due to his small frame and resemblance of a mouse. Hendrik had been lucky. He'd managed to get on a team with Dover. The other boy on Hendrik's team was named Carver. He had dark hair and a firm look of determination.

Willow was on a team with James and a large-framed boy named Greg.

Grace waved the others to huddle up. "Since we're already facing a disadvantage, we need to be smart about this."

Nick scratched his head. "What do you mean? Each team has three people except us. We have an extra."

Grace gave a glace in Tam's direction. "Yes, an extra disadvantage. She's a Sparrow."

Nick nodded. "Gotcha."

"Hey," Tam objected. "What's that supposed to —"

"Like I was saying," Grace cut in. "We need to play smart." She pulled Nick and Creed

closer and spoke in a low tone. Tam struggled to hear. As she strained her ears, Tam glanced down at the forest below. The sun was just dipping below the horizon, casting shadows across the leaves and trees. If their team was up soon, they could possibly use the shadows to their advantage. Anything to draw the eye of the kapros would be useful. She bit her lip and took a deep breath. Tam felt like she had the most to prove tonight; plus, she really didn't want latrine duty.

"Shouldn't you be planning your strategy with your team?" Hendrik asked as he came to stand next to her. Without realizing it, she'd walked away from her whispering teammates. Great, this was all she needed—to give Hendrik more ammo to make fun of her. Tam glanced up at him, expecting to see a smirk on his face. Instead, his eyes looked serious. "Grace can be a jerk sometimes."

"Yeah, no kidding."

"Don't worry, Sticks. You got this."

"Sticks? Really? Do you still need to call me that?"

"Sorry," he said with a goofy grin.

"Better get back to your team. I bet they're lost without you."

Hendrik nodded. "Yeah. I mean no, but yeah, I should get back to my team. Good luck, Sticks."

Tam's ears burned, and she spun toward him. But he was already striding away. She muttered under her breath before rejoining Grace and the others.

"Okay, Pam, so this is what we have so far-"

"Tam," she corrected.

Grace waved away her comment and continued. "Whatever. Anyway, I think your skill will best serve as a distraction. Being docked the five minutes might be worth it if we are able to snatch the flag while the kapros is focused on you. It won't see us coming, and we can be in and out in seconds. Got it, Pam?"

Before Tam could answer, her team was walking toward Cassia to tell her they were ready. They wanted her to be a distraction? That was just great. She would get to look like a fool while her team took all the credit and glory. If they weren't going to take her seriously, she would have to show them she deserved to be there just as much as they did. Even if it meant taking some risks.

Chapter Nine

Tam's team had the advantage of going last. They would be able to watch the others and avoid costly mistakes. The first team was Hendrik's team. They took nearly twenty minutes, carefully moving only when the animal was distracted and using the wind as a tool to lure the kapros toward their scent and away from Dover. Once the animal was far enough away, Dover moved silently to the flag and back. They hadn't been seen, so no time was added, but they had moved so slowly they might have a chance to beat them if they went with Grace's plan. The second team was fortunate, and the kapros was rooting around on the other side of the arena when they started out. Maybe this wouldn't be so difficult after all.

Grace was busy showing off her new gear to the others on their team while Tam watched.

"Shouldn't you be paying attention too?" Tam asked, but the girl ignored her.

Turning her attention back to the forest floor, Tam held her breath as Greg, the boy with broad shoulders, lowered himself to the ground. There was still a large open space between him and the flag. Glancing nervously in the direction of the boar, he hunched low and prepared to run for it. James clung to a nearby tree while Willow stationed herself closer to the kapros, presumably to cause a distraction if it were alerted to his presence.

Taking a deep breath, the boy took off toward the flag at full speed. Tam was impressed. His steps barely made any sound as he ran. She glanced back toward the kapros. Wait, where did it go? Her eyes searched the brush where it should have been.

Tam's breath caught in her throat as a huge, furry mass sprang toward the boy. The two teammates hidden in the trees on the far side shouted in a panic and threw rocks, but the kapros was completely focused on its target. He wasn't going to make it. Willow tried to call out as a distraction, but the creature was singularly focused on Greg.

Snorting and snarling, it moved faster than Tam knew possible. Cassia yelled something next to her ear. Immediately, a rope shot down in front of the boy. He ran to it with outstretched fingers.

"Come on, come on …" Cassia muttered.

Just as his fingers grasped the knotted end, Greg was yanked up so fast Tam was sure he would have whiplash. The boar let out a frustrated growl as he was pulled out of reach just before it could clamp onto the boy's leg.

Tam let out her breath in a whoosh and stepped back from the rail. It was a good thing Pathfinders had been positioned at various locations above, or he would have been a goner for sure. But no trees were over that particular spot. Curious, she glanced up. A sturdy rope had been positioned over the clearing, and a Pathfinder hung from it on a harness. They must have a powerful grappler to get one to go that far. Craning her neck, Tam spotted a large machine the rope had been launched from. She hadn't noticed it being shot in all the commotion.

Grace was also staring at the enormous grappler. Pulling the others on her team close, she began babbling excitedly. Tam leaned in to hear what they were talking about.

"See, it will work perfectly." Grace pulled her grappler out of her pack just enough for the others huddled around her to see. "This is no ordinary grappling gun either. It shoots twice as far, and it's twice as accurate. All we need to do is shoot the tree with the flags, zip over, and drop down and grab it. We never even have to touch the forest floor."

"Whoa, that's an awesome idea!" Creed exclaimed.

Nick nodded. "But how did you get one of those already? And is that considered cheating?"

"My family has connections," Grace said with a grin. "And no way. Cassia never said we couldn't use grapplers on this drill."

Tam sighed. "That's because she didn't know you had one. And that's a really long shot. Even if your gun could shoot it that far, would it hit the tree with enough power to really stick?"

Grace narrowed her eyes. "You think I would suggest it if I didn't think it would hold? Of course, it will stick. Don't be such a little nestling. Leave it to me. Don't worry about anything other than creating that distraction. Remember, we *want* the kapros to see you."

Tam sighed. After watching it take off after that boy, she was even less excited about this idea.

Greg was back at the platform being checked out by a medic now. Their team's run had ended in defeat. His face was ashen, and his hands shook visibly. His broad frame seemed to have shrunk into a hunched-over mass. He looked like a little boy afraid of the monsters under his bed. But these monsters were real, and they were everywhere.

Rain began to fall around them as they put on their gear and prepared for their run. Tam still wanted to prove herself, but with this plan, she was going to look like the idiot that got spotted. Or even worse, she could be the idiot that got gored. Maybe Tam could keep to the trees and still gain the animal's attention. It wouldn't be nearly as dangerous then. And even if she looked like a fool in front of everyone, being on the winning team would help counteract it, right? The bark on the tree felt cool and damp under her touch. This rain was going to make things harder. If she didn't watch out, she could easily slip.

Tam climbed the tree and waited for the signal to start. The others were in position too. Cassia raised her hand, then dropped it to indicate it was time. Penny leapt from the first tree to the second, taking care to make sure to plant her tree claws firmly in the bark. Grace took off ahead with Nick and Creed at her heels. Tam made her way to the right side of the arena and waited for Grace to reach the edge of the clearing. It was difficult to make her out through the branches, and she'd lost track of the other two completely.

Dropping down a few feet to get a better look, she scanned the tress for movement and saw Grace had reached the clearing. But how was she supposed to know when to make a distraction? They hadn't gone over that part. Now where was that kapros? She didn't want it to take her by surprise. Tam finally spotted the furry mass almost directly below the flags. That was bad luck. Or maybe it was good in their case. It would take the kapros longer to reach Tam, and that would hopefully allow Grace enough time to grab the flag and get back to safety.

Tam jumped to the next tree to get in position and gasped as her foot slid on the wet bark. Luckily, her other spikes were firmly planted, and she was able to recover. It was a good reminder to watch her step before calling that thing over.

Thwap.

With wide eyes, Tam realized Grace had already shot the grappler. The kapros raced to the tree and paced around it, grunting with excitement. Without thinking, Tam dropped to the forest floor and began to shout. Would it be too late to get its attention? Nope. Apparently, a human voice trumped the clunk of metal hitting wood. Spinning around, the creature darted toward her. Taking a step back, she realized it would be upon her in seconds. This hadn't been part of her plan.

Slamming her claws into the nearest tree, she began to climb. That thing was at least five feet tall. She would have to move fast. Tam cried out in dismay as her claw glanced off the tree and the other broke loose, tearing the bark off with it. Her feet slid, looking for purchase, but she'd already slipped back to the ground. Lashing out wildly, Tam tried again but couldn't seem to get her claws to stick.

She willed herself not to look back but couldn't resist a peek. The creature was right behind her now. Tam dodged to the side just as it slammed into the tree where she'd been moments before. It seemed momentarily dazed. Taking aim, she leapt to another tree. This time, her claws stuck, and she scrambled upward. Gasping, Tam sat down on a branch and stared down at the enraged kapros who had just lost his meal.

A scream startled her so much she almost slipped again. Grace was falling. The grappler had gotten her part of the way there but must have not gone into the tree deep enough to hold until she reached the other side. Tam searched above for any sign of the two Pathfinders. To her dismay, they were both positioned near her. They must have been coming to her aid, and now they were nowhere near Grace who lay on the ground unmoving. "Get to the platform!" one of the Pathfinders yelled as they swooped by, heading toward Grace.

Grace was too far away. There was no way they would get there in time and nothing she could do either. Unless ... They weren't supposed to engage the animal in combat, but there was no other option. Snatching her bow from her back, Tam pulled back an arrow as far as she could and let it fly. To her amazement, it hit the target, causing the boar to let out a high-pitched squeal and spin around in circles. Wincing, she covered her ear with one hand and gripped the tree with the one that still held the bow. Under her fingertips, the tree began to shake. An earthquake? That was all they needed. The shaking increased until she had to wrap both arms around the tree to keep from falling.

It was her turn to scream as the fence was ripped apart under the feet of a dozen or more full-sized kapros. Tam was completely frozen to the spot as she watched in horror the scene below. The boars were destroying everything in their paths, including the trees. A hand gripped her shoulder, bringing her back to the danger of her own situation.

"Follow me. Now!" Cassia ordered. Tam obeyed and kept right behind Cassia all the way back to the platform. Willow embraced her, and Hendrik and Dover gathered around.

"What ... what happened? Why did that stampede charge in?"

Hendrik shook his head "Did you forget? When a baby kapros is injured, it's defense mechanism is to call for help."

"Oh." Tam's face fell. "Then this is all my fault." Suddenly she remembered her reason for shooting that arrow. "Grace! Is she ..." Tam searched the forest floor below, but it was a mass of destruction and brown furry beasts.

"She's okay," Willow said, pointing to the platform where Grace sat stunned. Relieved, Tam turned back to the railing. Below, the Pathfinders both dropped to the ground, fired several shots into the mass of kapros, then leapt back into the trees. The boars let out angry squeals and followed them deeper into the forest and away from the community.

"Everyone head back to camp immediately," Cassia ordered.

Tam's throat was completely dry as they followed her across the return zip line and back to the main base. Everyone on her team received a harsh reprimand and were told they were to be confined to the barracks for two days except for training and meals. They were also on latrine duty until further notice, and they had to personally assist in the cleanup of sector five. All in all, it wasn't as bad as it could have been. Tam half expected to be kicked out after they all screwed up so badly, but Cassia seemed to think the scare they received was punishment enough.

As they began to head back to the barracks, Tam felt a tap on her shoulder. It was Grace. Great. Now she was going to get chewed out all over again.

"Um ... Hey, Tam."

"What's up?" At least she'd gotten her name right this time.

Grace sighed. "Do I have to say it?"

"Say what?"

"Ugh." She looked away. "Thanks. There, I said it."

Tam was taken aback. Did she hear that right?

"Even though it was a stupid thing to do, what you did saved my life. But don't let it go to your head or anything. I still think you're a screw up, and come tomorrow, my squad is back in action, and no more of this being nice to you stuff."

"You were being nice?"

Grace merely scowled and walked away.

And Grace kept to her word. She seemed even more of a jerk over the next few days. Almost like she had something to prove. Tam was glad when their punishment was over, and they were allowed some time off to go home and spend some time with their families before their first big mission.

Tam sat at the table with her father eating dinner and filling him in on all she'd learned. This was the first time they'd been able to visit since she began training. Feeling full from the big meal he'd prepared, she leaned back in her seat.

"Do you know your mission yet?" Tam's dad asked.

"No, they won't tell us until tomorrow. Do you remember your first mission?"

Dad got a far-off look in his eyes. "Like it was yesterday. My squad consisted of me, your mother, and our friend, Tom."

Tam leaned forward, anxious to hear every detail. "What were you supposed to do?"

"Well it was supposed to be a quick mission. We were told to deliver supplies to some Pathfinders stationed a few miles away. The first half of the mission went great, but on the way home, it got dark, and we lost our way. We ended up having to survive out there for three days until we were found by a search team. It was so embarrassing. From that moment on, your mom was a woman on a mission to prove she wasn't a screw up. It lit a fire under her, and she quickly climbed the ranks."

"Wow, that was quite the first mission." Tam laughed.

Dad let out a low chuckle. "It sure was." He picked up a plate he'd been filling and handed it to Tam. "Here, take this to your grandma."

Tam climbed the steps to Gran's room. She was surprised to find her sitting in a chair by the window. Her eyes lit up when she saw Tam.

"Hi Gran. You look like you're feeling better. I brought you some food."

"Thank you, Mary."

Gran sometimes got her confused with the girl who used to come babysit when Tam was a baby. Mary something or other.

"Gran, it's me, Tam."

She nodded. "Tam? Why yes, that's my granddaughter. Such a lovely baby."

Tam shook her head. "I'm not a baby anymore. I've grown up. And guess what? I'm becoming a Pathfinder now."

"A Pathfinder?" Grandma began to shake. "No! Oh no! Too dangerous. The kapros are everywhere. The world isn't safe since the experiment."

"Experiment? What do you mean, Gran?"

"The experiment that made the monsters. Have you seen my keys?" she asked suddenly. "I need my keys."

Tam was intrigued. She'd known Gran was around before the famine and wars caused by the kapros, but she could never get her to speak of it. Could Gran know something about how it all began?

"I'll help you find your keys if you tell me more about the kapros." She glanced around the room. Gran had a set of what looked like janitor keys that she liked to keep under her pillow. They were old and didn't fit any locks around the house, but she treasured them all the same. Flipping over the pillow, sure enough, there they were. Tam handed them to her grandma.

"Now, what can you tell me about the experiment?"

Gran snatched her keys and held them to her chest. A look of recognition came over her face. "Hi, Tamerelda!"

"Hi, Gran. Can you tell me about the experiment now?"

"The experiment? Hmmm ..." She thought for a moment, scratching her chin. Then pointed to her bed.

"You want me to help you back into bed?" Tam grabbed Gran's elbow to help her stand, but she shook her head.

"No, I need my box." She pointed again, this time aiming her finger lower. Could Gran mean under the bed? Tam got on her hands and knees and peered underneath. A dark box was wedged against the wall. Reaching under, she pulled it out, coughing at the sudden dust storm the motion produced.

"This?" she asked, holding it up.

The woman nodded. "Yes, it's time." Her voice seemed stronger somehow. Louder and clear. Tam dusted off the dark, metal box and placed it on Gran's lap. It had a keyhole in the front. Gran held up her keyring and selected one with a rounded top, then put it in the box and twisted. The lock opened with a soft click. Reaching inside, she pulled out a leather book and placed it in her great-granddaughter's hands.

As Tam started to take the book, Gran grabbed her hand in hers and held tight. Her eyes met Tam's. They were fervent, pleading. "Please forgive me."

"Forgive you for what?" But the woman's eyes had glazed back over. "Gran? Grandma?"

"Mary? Mary, don't just stand there. The baby is crying. Go feed the baby."

Saying her goodbyes, Tam slipped to her room and sat on the bed. She stared down at the book for several minutes. It was silly to be nervous. The book probably just contained a bunch of old recipes or something. And yet she couldn't get that look Gran had on her face out of her head. And those words. Please forgive her? Forgive her for what? Not sharing her blueberry pie recipe sooner? With a resigned huff, Tam opened the book. The handwriting was difficult to read, and there were dozens of symbols she didn't understand. Was it some kind of scientific journal? Several loose notes were also stuffed between the pages along with a photograph of four people in white lab coats. The woman on the far right caught her attention.

"Gran?" She was much younger, maybe only in her early twenties, but Tam recognized her eyes and the cowlick in the front of her hair. She flipped the photo over. On the back it read, 'Denton, 2035.' Wow, Tam thought. 2035? That was almost 80 years ago!

And Denton? Why did that name seem familiar? Maybe Gran had mentioned the name before. She flipped to the next page and read aloud. "May 3rd, 2035: Today, we have been commissioned to eliminate the muuagi plant. A fast-growing vine that emits poison gasses when disturbed. The plant has already spread to many locations and is actively killing crops and forests. The question of how to remove it on a massive scale without disturbing wildlife or local inhabitants will be the real challenge. However, I am confident my team is up to the task. Authorities have asked us to keep experiments top secret, as rumors of an unstoppable vine may cause national panic."

On the following page was a hand drawn picture of a spikey plant with a flower in the center and vines stemming from the base. Underneath was the title, 'Muuagi plant.'

She read the footnotes on the side aloud. "Noxious, non-indigenous vine. Mix of unspecified jungle plant and northwestern vine. Fast growing. Destroys all local plant life. Known weakness: none."

Scratching her head, Tam wondered what these vines might have to do with the kapros.

Dad's voice drifted up the stairs. "Don't you need to get back before curfew?"

Curfew, right. She'd almost forgotten. All new recruits were supposed to be in the base camp by ten o'clock. According to the clock on the wall, it was nearly nine thirty. She'd better get going. Tam placed the photo back in the book and closed it. Tucking it under her arm, she went downstairs.

"Good luck," her dad said, embracing her in a big hug. He wasn't usually much of a hugger, so it took her by surprise. "And please—"he held her arms and looked straight into her eyes" —be careful."

Tam nodded. "I will."

That night, she waited until everyone was asleep before pulling the book out again and lighting a candle. She thumbed through the notes, stopping at the drawing of a wild boar. According to the footnotes, their hearty stomachs and natural ability to dig up roots made boars the perfect candidates to rid forests of the invasive weed. Tests were still needed to make them faster and stronger, so they would be more effective, and the poisonous vines wouldn't make them sick. The boars were injected with a drug called canazole.

She flipped to the next page. It read, "Initial results promising. Swine shows no distress when exposed to gas, radiation, and poison. Animals have doubled in size, have far reduced gestational periods, and are reproducing quickly. End of world hunger? We have dubbed these new creatures, kapros."

The next entry was dated a week later. It read, "We set them loose in the forest today. Everything going marvelously, but kapros quickly become fatigued and full. Vines are still spreading faster than boars can destroy. Perhaps a higher dose?"

For the next several pages, the book was filled with equations and the names of compounds and chemicals. Finally, she found another entry.

It was dated May 24th, "Today, we added the experimental form of adrenaline and steroid compound to the formula and administered it to the kapros. Not much change. Will keep in outdoor enclosure overnight and re-test tomorrow."

Anxious to see the results, Tam flipped to the next page. Some of the writing was written so quickly, she couldn't make it out. She skipped down a few sentences and read, "Outdoor enclosure empty. Torn apart by some kind of animal. Perhaps a predator? Fredrick and Lopez are searching nearby forest for any sign."

The next entry was the following day. "Fredrick is dead, and Lopez is gravely injured. Kapros appetite insatiable. What have we done?"

Tam turned the page again, but the next several pages were illegible. She could pick out a few words here and there, but it seemed obvious the writer was either in distress or in a hurry at the time they wrote it. She flipped through the rest of the book, but the next couple pages were the same. After that, it was blank.

Tam's mouth went dry, and her hands shook. She knew the rest. Famine, wars, years of trying to survive. And her grandma ... that sweet, crazy old lady was one of the people responsible. Gran had been one of the scientists. How was this possible, and why hadn't she said anything all these years? Why now? Her mind buzzed with unanswered questions. Her sweet, innocent grandma was a villain. If it wasn't for her, maybe none of this would have happened. No, no she was a victim of circumstances. Wasn't she? Tam didn't know how to feel or what to think.

Grace sat up in bed from across the room. "Hey, do you mind? There are people trying to sleep in here. Quit mumbling and put out that light."

Hardly hearing her, Tam absently blew out the candle. She didn't know if she should tell someone about this or not. What would it really change other than giving them a scapegoat for the problems of the past eighty years? Would they try to punish Gran? Put her to death? Even if she did start this, the woman didn't deserve to be raked over the coals. She needed time to think. Tucking the book under her pillow, Tam resolved to find a place to hide it in the morning.

Rolling over, a sinking feeling settled into the pit of her stomach. The new information made everything feel even more real and dangerous. The kapros weren't just some overgrown pigs. No, they were genetically modified eating, killing machines. They weren't just a part of the famine or wars. They caused it the famine and wars. And Gran ... Gran created them.

The next day, Tam awoke to the sound of a bell clanging outside.

"You're not up yet?" Willow appeared back in the room, fully dressed, with her pack slung over her shoulder. "Come on, Tam. Hurry!" she urged. "Today is the day!"

"I'm up. I'm up. Just mentally preparing."

Willow rolled her eyes. "Well, mentally prepare while you get dressed. See you down there." And with that, her friend dashed off. Such a flighty little thing.

Sitting up on the edge of her bed, Tam stretched. She needed to get her head back in the game. This stuff with the experiment could wait. Like Willow said, today was the day.

By the time she got dressed and came outside, all the other fledglings were already lined up, listening to commander Cassia. Tam tried to sneak unnoticed into a spot on the end next to Hendrik.

Cassia cleared her throat and raised an eyebrow in Tam's direction. "As I was saying, today you will get your assignments from the climbing wall. There are flags positioned all over the wall. The team with the most flags at the end of five minutes will receive the most challenging mission. The team with the second highest will receive the next mission, and the team with the fewest will get the easiest mission. This way it will help ensure the weakest team doesn't get in over their heads, and the strongest team will have a challenge."

Tam gazed up at the wall, already planning her route.

"Do you think it's worth it?" Hendrik whispered. "Do we really want the biggest challenge?"

"Oh, and one more thing," Cassia said, holding her hands up for silence. "The team with the most points will also get one leisure day a week for the next month, plus twenty credits to spend however they choose."

Excited chatter rose up all around them. A day off every week? That would be amazing. All this training was already taking a toll on Tam's body.

Casia held up her hands again. "The flags toward the top are worth more points than those near the bottom. Blue flags are five, red flags ten, and black flags are worth twenty. Additionally, there is one golden flag at the very top that is worth fifty points."

Willow leaned over and whispered, "The gold flag could practically win the whole thing for us. We gotta get that one."

"Now, I'll give you a few moments to get ready and talk over your strategy as a team."

"Wait!" Grace held up her hand.

"Yes?"

"The teams aren't fair. Team A has an advantage because there are four of them." Grace crossed her arms and scowled at Tam. "Wonder whose fault that is?"

"I thought you said I put my team at a disadvantage," Tam said with a smirk.

Grace's scowl deepened, but she didn't have a ready retort.

"Oh yes, I forgot to mention," Cassia said to Tam's squad. "One of your team must sit out for this particular challenge. You can decide who as a team."

"You guys can go ahead. I don't mind sitting out," Willow chirped.

"Are you kidding?" Tam asked. "You're our best climber. We need you."

Dover and Hendrik agreed. Tam knew what she had to do. She was their weakest link and the reason they had too many people. "I'll sit out," she and Hendrik echoed at the same time.

"Really. You go ahead, Sticks."

Wincing at the nickname, she shook her head. The last thing Tam wanted was for Hendrik to do her any favors.

"I mean it, Tam. I pulled my arm yesterday during shoka training."

With a shrug, she conceded. "Okay, fine. I'll go. But *you* owe *me*."

Hendrik grinned. "Sure thing."

Why was that smile so infuriating? Probably because she got the feeling he expected her to melt at those dimples of his. If anything, it had the opposite effect. Well, okay they were a little cute, but anyone who was that conceded and thought calling a girl 'Sticks' was some sort of compliment was too obnoxious to swoon over.

"Okay, now let's figure out our plan," Dover said, waving them to come in closer.

"Any good ideas?" Tam asked.

"Yeah, I think so." Dover scratched his chin. "Willow, you're the fastest, so I think you should ignore all the other flags and go straight to the top for the gold flag, then get some black ones on the way down if you have extra time. Most people will probably go for the mid-level, so I'll go to the center between red and black and try to fend them off. Tam, the blue ones will probably be ignored, but they add up too. Grab as many blue as you can and then work your way up. Sound okay to everyone?"

Tam and Willow nodded.

"Good, let's show these nestlings what we've got."

Chapter Ten

As Tam waited for the signal, she wiped the sweat from her palms. Cassia held a pocket watch in her hand with her other arm raised. "Ready? Go!" As she spoke, Cassia brought her arm down. Tam leapt forward and grabbed the wall with both hands, pulling herself up to the first flag and snatching it. Then, instead of continuing up, she went to the left, getting as many blue flags as possible and stuffing them in the satchel they provided. Dover had been right. Practically no one was trying for the blue ones. Willow was nearly halfway up already. Tam couldn't see Dover but didn't have time to keep looking. She zagged back to the right, keeping a steady pace. A pain shot through her fingertips as a shoe pressed down directly on them.

"Oh, sorry about that," Grace said from above her and twisted her foot before stepping off. Tam yelled and slipped from the wall, falling about ten feet and landing flat on her back. She gasped for breath as Hendrik rushed over.

"Are you alright?"

"I'm ... I'm fine," she said with a wheeze.

"Let me see your fingers."

"Really, I'm all right." Snatching her hand away, Tam ran back to the wall. Her fingers were throbbing, but she ignored the pain and climbed straight back up, grabbing a few missed flags along the way.

"One more minute!" Cassia shouted.

What? How did that go so fast? Tam reached the spot where she'd fallen and continued her pattern, trying to move double time.

"Thirty seconds!"

Tam grabbed another flag and another, lost her footing for a moment but recovered. One more flag was just out of reach. She'd have to jump to the next handhold to grab it, but if she missed, she'd fall for sure, and it was a long way down.

Just.

One.

More.

Tam leapt, grabbing the handhold by her fingertips. Her legs dangled as she struggled to hang on. Grunting with effort, Tam lifted herself just enough to get a foothold and snatched the flag.

"Time's up!" Cassia yelled. "Come on down."

By the time Tam got back down to the floor, the muscles in her arms were shaking. Only then did she allow herself to look at her fingers. They were an angry shade of red and two of them were already turning purple.

"What's your problem?" Hendrik looked furious.

Confused, Tam stuttered. "W-what?

But Henrik strode past her and faced Grace. "You did that on purpose. She could have broken her neck."

Grace held up her hands. "It wasn't my fault. She put her fingers right under my foot."

"Gimme a break. I saw you stomp down."

Cassia pulled Hendrik back. "Calm down."

"But-"

"Control yourself, recruit, or you'll earn latrine duty."

Hendrik straightened up. "Yes ma'am."

"Now, open your bags, and let's count the flags."

The teams were running fairly even. It looked like it would be just a matter of a few points. "Oh, actually one more," Willow said, producing the gold flag.

"You got it!" Dover gave her a high five. "Why didn't you lead with that one?"

"Because ... suspense, silly. Makes it more interesting, don't you think?"

Tam rolled her eyes, just glad it was over.

"Congratulations," Cassia said. Grace's team had come in second place, and Brian's team last, but not by much. She handed each team their assignment, along with the twenty crowns to split among them. They went into the armory and plopped down around the table. Tam held a cold wet a cloth on her injured fingers. "Well, open it!" she urged Dover.

Tearing the seal, he unrolled the paper. "Take lunch to unit five? That's the challenging assignment? What do you think the easy one was, shine your commander's shoes?" Dover dropped the paper in disgust.

"Now, hang on, let's see the details." Tam examined the directions. "I think this unit is actually pretty far away. See, it even has a map. Plus, it says we have to spend the night out there and only eat what we can find. This could still be fun."

"Yeah, I suppose so. I guess I was hoping it would say we needed to bring back a kapros head or something."

Hendrik pointed at the bottom of the paper. "Actually, it says we are to avoid contact with a kapros under any circumstances."

"Still," Willow shrugged, "it will be exciting just to get outside of our little bubble, right?'

Dover nodded. "Yeah, I guess you're right. This is going to be epic, guys! What time do we need to leave?"

Tam smoothed out the paper. "It says we have to leave before noon so we won't be traveling at nightfall."

"Better get our things together then." Dover stood and turned toward the barracks. "You coming, Hendrik?"

"Yeah, I'm right behind you."

Tam grabbed Hendrik's wrist as he stood. Startled, he didn't even remember to flash his dimples. "Sorry," Tam's face grew red, and she let go. "I just wanted to say thanks for

"... you know. For standing up for me to Grace. You didn't have to, but it was a nice gesture."

"Of course. Not a big deal. I would have done it for Dover or Willow too."

Tam frowned. "Yeah, no. Of course you would have. I didn't think you meant anything by it."

"And don't let Grace bother you. She probably just feels threatened because you're faster and stronger."

"That's so not true."

"Cuter too," he said with a wink.

Goosebumps sprang up on Tam's arms, not entirely unpleasant. Before she could respond, he followed after Dover to the men's barracks.

"Oooh." Willow grinned. "Someone likes you."

Tam moved the cool cloth from her fingers to her burning cheeks. "Don't be silly. He flirts with all the girls. Doesn't mean anything. He just likes to tease me."

"He's never flirted with me."

"Okay, one exception. Stop smiling like that. We need to get ready to go." Tam slid the bench back from the table and made her way to their room. It didn't take long to pack up all they would need, especially since they were traveling light.

Tam checked her bag one last time, then they headed off toward the southern-most point of Aviary.

Dover checked the map and pointed. "We need to go that way first then veer toward the West."

Tam looked over his shoulder. "Why not just travel Southwest? Wouldn't that save time?"

Dover traced his finger from where they were on the map to the destination. "See any problem with that?"

"Oh," Tam felt dumb. "No trees."

"Yeah, at least not any close enough together. The Pathfinders have this route pretty well mapped out and update it every year or so when there's a big change. Not every tree is mapped out on here obviously, but it gives you a general idea of the thickness. We need to keep toward these heavily-treed areas."

"Alright, enough talking. Let's get this mission started!" Willow jumped from the edge of the platform to the nearest tree. Dover and Hendrik followed suit. Tam stood on the edge of the platform. The forest floor was so far down, but, at least there were no kapros in sight. She took a deep breath and jumped across the gap to join the others. Willow was already several trees ahead. Keeping up with her was going to be a challenge for all of them.

Because of her speed, Willow ended up being the natural leader. Dover would occasionally call for her to halt using the horn fastened to his chest and re-direct them to keep on course. Pretty soon, Tam got into a rhythm, and her nervousness started to fall away. Instead, she allowed herself to feel the rush of adrenaline every time she swung from a branch or leapt to the next point. As long as Tam jumped to the place Hendrik had just left, she knew it was a safe area to land. She was starting to get a good feel for her mother's tree claws. They worked great. Having something properly fitted to her hand cut down on her muscle fatigue dramatically, and the retractable, pressure sensing claws also made a very satisfying *THWIP* sound every time they stuck into a tree.

An hour or so later, Dover blew the horn again.

"What is it?" Willow asked.

"Let's take a short break and roost for a while. Not all of us have your stamina," Dover remarked.

Tam let herself come to rest on a branch, thankful for a chance to rest her aching muscles. Her arms throbbed with the exertion, and she rubbed her hands over them. Hendrik slouched down in the crook of a tree and closed his eyes.

"Sore?" Dover asked as he perched on a limb next to her.

"Not really …" Tam lied.

Tilting his head, Dover pursed his lips. "Really?"

"Okay, maybe a bit."

Dover reached into his pack and pulled out a small bottle. "Here, rub a little of this salve on your arms. It really helps take the edge off."

Tam took the bottle and opened it. "It smells horrible," she said, wrinkling her nose.

"Ah yes, well, my mom says the worse it smells, the better it heals."

"Then this stuff must be pretty amazing." Tam grinned. Dipping a couple fingers into the sticky solution, she was starting to doubt her decision to give it a try, but Dover was watching with a look of expectancy, so she scooped out a glob of the amber colored solution and rubbed it on her left arm. "Oh!" Tam exclaimed. The relief was almost instant. "This really is amazing. Is your mom a medic or something?"

"She's more of a natural healer. Likes to use leaves and junk."

Tam rubbed another small glob onto her other arm before handing the jar back to Dover.

"So, you didn't want to be a healer?"

Dover shook his head. "No, ever since I was young, I've wanted to be a Pathfinder. I'll be the first in my family. At first, my mom wasn't so keen on it. I'm an only child, and my dad died during that epidemic a couple years ago, so I'm all she has." Dover pulled out a brown, scuffed up pocketknife. "This was my dad's. My mom gave it to me after he died. I carry it everywhere. When I have it, I feel like part of him is with me. In a strange way, I think it makes my mom feel better. Almost like he's watching after me, you know?" He frowned and put the knife in his pack. "I think she understands now that this is my calling. I can help make our village a better place by using my talents as a Pathfinder."

"Exactly," Tam said with a nod. "My dad didn't want me to become one either, but he's better about it now. It's what I need to do."

"Yeah, my mom's gotten really supportive. She's put most of our savings into my training for the Pathfinder test, and now she's counting on me to make it to the end and become a full member. Pathfinders make good money, and I aim to take care of her."

"I'm sure you will. You're the most skilled among us."

"Hey, I heard that," Hendrik said, his eyes still closed. "And I'm highly offended. It may be true, but I'm still offended."

Dover laughed. "Well, thanks, but that's not true. Look at Willow. She's not even tired yet." Tam followed his gaze to her friend who was leaping back and forth between the same two trees as if getting impatient.

Willow caught them looking her way and said, "You guys done resting yet or what? Let's go!"

Tam snickered. "She is pretty energetic."

Dover pulled the map back out and studied it for a moment. "Before we move on, there should be a stream we can fill our canteens with around here."

Straining her ears, Tam noticed a trickling sound above the rustling of the leaves. She leapt to the next tree and peered down through the leaves. "There it is." Tam pointed to the narrow stream of water snaking through the rocks. A motion near the water's edge caught her eye. Pulling back a branch to get a better view, she froze. A furry, black body with a large snout rooted around at a patch of weeds.

Her friends had just joined her. By the look on their faces, they saw it too.

"Do you think it knows we're here?" Tam whispered.

Hendrik shook his head. "Not likely. We're downwind, plus they can't really look up, remember? In any case, we should move to another spot to get water."

"Nonsense," Dover said. "It's just a small one. Only six feet. I can take it easily. Then we can have pork chops for dinner."

Hendrik pursed his lips. "But what if it's not alone? There could be a whole sounder around here somewhere. Remember what happened during stealth training? I really don't think we should."

"I don't see any others, and I have a pretty clear view. Anyway, I'll kill it in one blow before it can make a sound. What do you think, Tam?"

"Well ... they did tell us to keep away from the kapros on this mission. But then again, it does seem to be alone."

"I don't know guys. I'm kinda with Hendrik on this one," Willow said with a frown. "But I'll have your back regardless."

"It will be fine," Dover said. "And think about the looks on the other trainees' faces when we bring back our first boar head."

"Guys, I really don't think we should," Hendrick said with a frown.

Tam could just see the look on Grace's face now. "Come on, a kapros kill on the first mission will make us legends," she said with a grin. "Let's do it."

Chapter Eleven

Tam, Hendrik, and Willow each spread out, forming a triangle around the beast. They were poised and ready to spring into action if Dover got into any trouble. Tam kept her bow firmly on her back this time, not confident enough in her skills to think she could hit it in the eye. And after what happened with the baby boar, she didn't even want to try. Instead, Tam kept her hand on her shoka.

Dover positioned himself above the kapros, his blade drawn. He planned to cut through the spinal column at the base of the neck like he'd done during the test. If he did it right, it would drop the beast fast.

Tam peered down at the boar's ugly face. Drool dripped from its mouth, and its nose twitched as it sniffed the air. Could it smell them? She said a silent prayer the animal would stay still so Dover could jump on top. What was taking him so long? She scanned the trees above the kapros, but Dover was nowhere in sight. Where had he gone? Before she had a chance to look closer, a shape dropped from behind the branches and down onto the animal. It let out an angry grunt and bucked like a bronco, running Tam's direction. Dover lay low, gripping the boar's dark fur and hanging on tight. How would he be able to stand and deliver a killing blow when he could barely stay on? The log hadn't moved like that during the test.

Tam gasped as the kapros raced beneath her, taking Dover with it. The boar kicked up dirt, and the sound of stomping hooves reverberated through the forest as it went by. Oh no. What had they done? What if it took Dover deep into the forest, and they couldn't find him again?

Turning, she jumped to the next tree and the next, trying to spot them below. Luckily, the boar seemed less concerned with getting away and more concerned with getting the thing off its back. With it jumping like that, Dover would never be able to make his move. Tam took a deep breath. Tam knew what she had to do. Carefully, she climbed down and dropped to the forest floor.

"Hey, pig, over here!" she shouted.

The kapros turned. His beady black eyes met hers. With a snort of rage, he stopped jumping and bolted toward her. Taking advantage of the distraction, Dover got to one knee, holding his shoka in one hand and gripping a tuft of fur in the other. He stood on shaky legs as the boar hurtled toward Tam. Lifting the shoka above his head, he brought it down with a sickening thud into the kapros's grisly neck. The boar let out a startled squeal. Tam jumped out of the way as the animal dropped and rolled, just missing her legs. Dover yelled as he flew from the creature and hit his back on a tree.

Once the kapros stopped rolling, it didn't get up again.

Willow and Hendrik dropped down next to Tam.

"Wow, he really did it!" Willow said.

Henrik's face was flushed. "We need to get back to the trees. This isn't safe."

Tam nodded. "Dover, are you okay?" she called. The boar had thrown him all the way across the clearing. He stood and gave a thumbs up.

Tam's eyes widened. Something moved behind Dover. It looked like a giant brown wall. "Guys ..."

Hendrik saw it too. "Dover, get out of there, now!"

Dover turned his head just as the head of a giant kapros appeared. It clamped its teeth down on Dover's shoulder. "NOOO!" Tam screamed. Another boar clamped down on Dover's leg. He screamed as the hog twisted, ripping his leg from his body.

Without thinking, Tam ran toward him. A pair of strong arms grabbed her from behind.

"It's too late. Tam, it's too late." The words barely registered as she fought against Hendrik. She elbowed him in the nose and sprang forward again. Hendrik wiped the blood from his face and tackled her from behind. Tam looked up just in time to see the look of horror frozen on Dover's face as more kapros sprang in to join the kill.

Willow was at her side now. She and Hendrik helped her to her feet and pulled her to the trees. "Climb," Willow whispered. "Now."

Several of the beasts had spotted them. With excited squeals, they dashed toward the trees. As if waking from a dream, Tam grabbed a low limb and climbed as fast as she could with the others right behind her. The tree shook as kapros rammed into it from below.

"They're in a frenzy now," Hendrik shouted. "We need to find something bigger." Another crash caused the tree to lurch to the side. Tam sprang away, barely getting a single claw in the next trunk. She stuck her boots into the bark and got a better grip. A yell came from below. Willow was hanging from a skinny branch. If she wasn't so small, there was no way it would hold. As it was, the limb bent under her weight, threatening to snap at any moment.

Tam scaled down, reaching out a hand. The tree shook, nearly knocking them both down. She reached again. Willow grabbed hold, and Tam swung her to the trunk where she was able to dig her claws in.

"Over here!" Hendrick called. A huge tree was just ahead. They jumped to it and scaled up higher and higher until the kapros lost their scent and headed in the other direction. The forest shook and swayed as they stampeded away.

Tam sat on branch and allowed herself to collapse into the rough bark of the tree. Angry tears leapt to her eyes. She should have helped. Should have done something. Why had Hendrik stopped her?

Hendrik perched next to her, placing his hand on her shoulder.

She shrugged it off and narrowed her eyes, hot tears streaming down her face. "Why did you stop me? I could have saved him."

He put his head in his hands and sighed, a look of misery on his face. "It was too late."

"It wasn't too late. I could have pulled him away, gotten him help." She wiped away her tears. "This is your fault, Hendrik."

Willow held up her hands, her own eyes puffy and red. "Come on, guys. This was no one's fault."

Hendrik's tone changed, and his eyes flashed. "I was the one who said we should find water somewhere else. I told you, but you didn't listen." He ran his fingers through his hair with frustration.

"Are you saying this is my fault?"

"No, I—"

Tam slapped him as hard as she could in the face. An angry welt instantly appeared. He looked back at her like a wounded animal. Without a word, he climbed up higher and jumped to the next tree.

Willow took a deep breath. "He's right, you know. If it wasn't for Hendrik, you'd be dead too."

When Tam didn't respond, Willow followed after Hendrik. Tam punched the tree and winced. Why would she take his side? She nursed her bloodied fist and stared down at the forest floor. Wanting to cry more but feeling numb, she sat there for what seemed like hours. The same horrible scene kept playing over and over in her head. His moment of triumph, his ripped apart body, and above all, his panicked eyes as life left them. Tam clenched her eyelids closed and shivered. What were they supposed to do now? Finishing such a small mission seemed ridiculous after the tragedy that just happened. Finally, Willow joined her again. "I think we should go. It's almost dark, and it won't be safe to travel much longer."

Tam just nodded. She was thirsty but pushed the feeling aside. They needed to press forward. Trying to focus all her energy and thought to climbing, she followed the others back toward Aviary. When they got to the spot Dover was attacked, her stomach churned. Dark red blood was spattered across the rocks below.

"Tam don't," Willow warned. But a morbid curiosity drew her down closer. There was no sign of his body, but she spotted the strap of his pack on a limb. Springing toward it, she gingerly lifted the pack. It was shredded and most of the contents had been strewn around in the brush. A glint of steel under a bush caught her eye. Reaching down, she picked up Dover's pocketknife and tucked it into her own pack before returning to the others. Hendrik gave a nod, and they continued toward home.

They traveled in silence, each lost in their own thoughts. The journey seemed even longer on the way back. Only a hint of daylight remained when they finally landed on the platform on the outskirts of the village.

"I'll tell them," Hendrik offered.

Willow shook her head. "We'll tell them together. Right, Tam?'

Tam nodded and followed them down the wooden pathways. They reached the gate far too soon. Now that they were back, Tam wished they were still in the trees. How could they face Commander Cassia and the others? Smitty looked confused at their arrival but opened the gate without a word after Hendrik gave the password.

They found Cassia in the main barracks by the senior officer's quarters. She sat enjoying a cup of something warm and laughing with the other officers. When Cassia saw them, she stood abruptly. "Why are you back?" Her voice seemed more concerned than angry.

"Can we, uh ... Can we talk to you outside?" Hendrik asked. He shuffled his feet and looked at the floor.

Cassia rose, and they followed her out the door. She listened with a stony face to our account of the tragedy. After Hendrik finished, she ran her fingers through her hair, her head bowed. When she brought her head back up, her face was flush. "So you're telling me that you deliberately went against orders, confronted a kapros, and got a member of your unit killed?" Her eyes flashed.

"Yes, ma'am," Tam murmured, "but the boar was small and all alone. We had no way of knowing, and we didn't think—"

"No, you didn't think!" Cassia's voice rose as she spoke. "Hendrik, I expected more from you of all people. Did you agree to go along with this too?"

Hendrik shifted his weight and glanced in my direction. "Yes."

"That's not true," Tam spoke up.

Hendrik waved her away. "Yes, it is. I went along with it, and now he's dead. I could have tried harder to stop him."

Cassia looked furious. "I don't want to hear it! Of all the irresponsible, foolish, idiotic things ..." Several curious onlookers were gathering nearby, drawn by the commotion. Cassia lowered her voice and narrowed her eyes. "Go wait in your rooms," she said through tight lips. "I'll have to talk to the general. Do not leave your bunks under any circumstances." Waving down a couple of officers, she barked orders for them to escort the trainees to their bunks.

The bunkhouse was especially quiet since everyone else was still on their missions. Well, almost everyone. Grace was sitting on her bed reading a novel. Her team must have finished their mission early. She put it aside when they walked in.

"What are you guys doing back so soon? No way you're done. I heard you got an overnight assignment."

Tam ignored her and laid down, pulling the blanket up over her head. She couldn't deal with Grace right now.

Willow sat across from her. "We, uh, ran into a bit of trouble."

"What kind of trouble?"

"Dover, he … Well—"

"Quiet, Willow," Tam said, more forcefully than she meant to.

Grace plopped down on Tam's bed and ripped the covers from her head. "What happened out there, Johansson?"

Tam sat up. Her eyes burned with fresh tears, and she quickly brushed them away.

Grace's features changed from angry to scared. "Tell me."

Tam pulled the covers back over her. "He's dead."

Chapter Twelve

General Kaan paced back and forth in front of Tam, Hendrick, and Willow at the emergency meeting that had been called. They each kept their heads bowed as they waited to hear their punishment for disobeying orders. Tam stared at a knothole on the plank beneath her, imagining it being a great swirling eye. She could barely stand the scrutiny of it. Finally, the general spoke, but Tam only picked up pieces of his speech. The words, disappointed and reckless, stood out to her. The swirling, judgmental eye felt like it was boring into her soul.

Reaching into her pocket, her fingers touched the cool metal of Dover's pocketknife and gripped the rough wooden handle. A lump formed in her throat as she regarded the eye on the floor, and it observed her in return. This was all her fault. She could have talked him out of it. Tam didn't raise her head until Willow grabbed her arm.

"Come on," she whispered and pulled Tam toward the door.

Tam followed Hendrik and Willow to the bunkhouse. "Wait, where are we going?'

"We're packing up our stuff and going home," Willow said with a sigh. "Didn't you hear General Kaan? We're on probation."

Tam shook her head. "For how long?"

Hendrik's eyes met hers, then looked away. "He didn't say," he said with a grunt. "Maybe permanently."

"Hendrik, I—" Tam reached toward Hendrik's shoulder. He shrugged it off and strode through the door.

"Save it," he said as he disappeared inside.

When Tam got home, it was nearly morning. She headed upstairs, hoping to get a couple hours of sleep before facing her father.

"Tamerelda." Her father's voice at the foot of the stairs made her jump.

"Oh, I thought you'd be asleep. Did Cassia come talk to you? I'm sorry if she woke you up." Tears sprang to her eyes. "I can explain everything … I—"

Her dad gathered her up in a bear hug, cutting her off. Tam sobbed into his shoulder. "Oh Dad, it was horrible."

"Shhh. I know. I know." He pet her hair awkwardly and held her in silence for a few moments. When he stepped back, he glanced away. "I uh … I made you some tea."

"Aren't you mad?"

He spoke just above a whisper. "I'm furious, but any explanation can wait until tomorrow. You've had a long traumatic day, and you need rest. Come," he said and led her to her room with the tea in his other hand. She sat down on the bed, and he tucked her in. Tam couldn't remember the last time he'd done that.

"Here," he said, handing her the mug. "Get some rest, Tamerelda." He paused at the door. "And welcome home."

Tam set the tea aside and burrowed down under her covers, trying in vain to fight back an onslaught of tears. A restless sleep followed, full of terrible dreams where she had to watch as, one by one, each of her friends were torn apart by a huge stampede of kapros as she stood watching, unable to move. She saw her father's face last. He didn't look scared or even in distress. As the kapros tore him to bits, he just stared at her with sad, unblinking eyes. The next two nights were similar. The details of the dreams changed, but each time, it ended the same—with someone she cared about ripped to shreds.

Tam sat up with a start after her latest dream. Sweat trickled down her back as she glanced out the window. *What time was it?* From the look of the sun, it was nearly noon. As she made her way downstairs, there was a sharp rap at the door.

"Tam, are you in there?"

Rubbing her eyes, Tam opened the door to see her friend, Elnor, standing outside, grinning.

"Hey, Tam. So, it's true. You're really back!"

Tam groaned. "Yeah, it's true."

"Your dad sent me to find you. He said he needs your help with the birds, and you've already slept half the day away."

Tam had been moping around the house for the last couple days, not even setting foot outside. Dad had told her last night that he wanted her to help with chores again. He said it would do her some good to keep her mind busy. Tam wasn't so sure.

"Alright, Elnor. Just give me a minute to get dressed." Tam ran back up to her room and changed into fresh clothes. As she pulled on her pants, she felt a weight in one of the pockets. Reaching inside, her fingers grasped a small object. The knife. Suddenly, Tam knew what she needed to do that day. Grabbing Gran's notebook from under her pillow, she stuffed it in her jacket pocket, not wanting to risk her dad finding it if he came in and tidied up the room. Something compelled her to keep it a secret for now. When she came downstairs, Elnor was eating the cold porridge on the table presumably left for Tam.

"Oh, I hope you don't mind. I didn't have much for lunch."

Tam pursed her lips. "It's fine. I'll just take something with me." She grabbed an apple and started for the door.

"Ooh, an apple sounds great. Got another?"

As they walked along with Elnor munching on the last apple, Tam ran her fingers over the railing, lost in her own thoughts.

"So, what happened?" Elnor asked between bites. "I heard someone died. Did someone die?"

Tam nodded.

"Whoa. Did you know them? Were you there? What does a kapros look like up close?"

Not wanting to get into it for fear of crying all over again, Tam ignored the question. "Don't you need to get back to the bakery?" she asked instead.

Elnor wrinkled her nose. "Oh yeah, you're right." She gave Tam a hug, then gave her a curious look. "You seem … different. Are you alright?"

Tam tried to give a reassuring smile. "I'm fine. Don't worry about it."

Elnor grinned. "Well, I'm so glad you're home anyway. I've really missed you. We'll talk later, okay? I've got so many questions. I want to hear about everything."

"Yeah, okay. I'll see you around." Tam waved as her friend climbed a ladder to the upper platform. Everyone kept saying how glad they were she was home, but was she home for good? Was this really the end of her journey as a Pathfinder? Tam leaned against a tree and gazed down at the forest floor, wondering how Willow and Hendrik were doing.

Her face grew hot, remembering how horribly she'd treated Hendrik. He was right all along. How could she show her face around him again? He was hardly speaking to her now. She would have thought the silence between them would be a welcome respite, but part of her—a bigger part than she'd like to admit—missed his attention and silly winks already and feared things had changed between them for good. "Ugh," Tam grunted and slid down the bark of the tree. Everything felt so backward. This was not how things were supposed to go. Her journey had ended before it even began. How could she go back to life as a Keeper after tasting the freedom of the wilds?

Tam shook herself, remembering that Dad was still waiting for her. Looked like he'd gotten what he wanted. She'd be a Keeper forever. A nice, safe job with no surprises as is fitting for a Sparrow. Pausing with her hand on the railing, she reached into her pocket and felt the cool steel of Dover's pocketknife again. Her mind was made up. Dad would just have to wait a little longer. She had something to do first before she lost her nerve. Spinning around, Tam headed in the opposite direction.

Dover was from the Hawk district. His mom would have already received the news by now. The poor woman must be devastated. Dover's last moments kept replaying in her head as she walked. Would she ever get the images out? Tam continued walking for several minutes after arriving in Hawk district as if in a daze, not knowing exactly where to go. The houses here were larger than those in the other districts. Most were several platforms tall and solidly built, unlike the homes in Sparrow that looked like they'd been pieced together with leftover wood scraps.

After wandering around aimlessly for a little longer, she asked around and got directions to Dover's home. Tam faltered when his house came into view. Maybe this was a bad idea. How could she face his mom with all the guilt and shame she had inside? The woman would know it was Tam's fault with one glance. What if his mom fell apart in front of her? Could Tam handle that? Or worse yet, what if his mom was furious? She was about to leave but stopped herself. No, Dover would want this, and she'd come this far.

Clenching her fists, Tam strode up to the door and gave a tentative knock. When no one answered, she gave a sigh of relief. Maybe it was for the best. She turned away, then stopped as the door creaked open behind her. A girl a little older than herself stood in the entrance.

"Hi, I'm … Um, I'm Tam. I'm looking for Mrs. Riggs. Is this the right house?"

The girl nodded. "Yes, this is her home. I'm Deena. I've been looking after her since … well, since the news of her son came."

"I see." Tam swallowed. "I'm a friend, I mean, I was a friend of Dover's. Can I maybe leave something for her?"

Deena stood aside and motioned for her to come in. "Why don't you come in and see her yourself. It might be good for her to see a friendly face."

Tam stepped inside and followed the girl through a tidy kitchen and into a cozy room with a fireplace. In front of the fire sat Dover's mom. Tam realized she had seen her a couple of times in the market, but she looked different now. Older somehow. Tired. It was amazing how much a change in demeanor could make in a person's features. Her usually cheerful, rosy face was gaunt and blank. Her friendly attitude had vanished. The woman didn't even seem to notice Tam come in. She sat slumped in her chair, and her hair hung limply around her face. What struck Tam the most was the woman's eyes. There was no expression in them at all. It was as if she were in a trance.

"This is Tam," Deena said. "She was a friend of Dover's." The woman didn't seem to hear. "Why don't you sit down, Tam." Deena motioned to a seat across from Dover's mom.

The chair let out a soft creak as Tam lowered herself into it. Despite the roaring fire in front of her, Tam shivered.

"I'll get you some cookies," Deena offered cheerfully and left the room.

They sat in silence for a few moments. Tam clasping and unclasping her hands. Finally, she broke the silence. "I ... um ... I'm sorry about Dover. He was a great guy." Nothing else she could think of seemed like the appropriate thing to say.

The woman still stared into the fire. Tam took a deep breath and pulled the knife from her pocket. "I was with Dover ... Um, I was with him when it happened. I'm sorry I couldn't stop it. I ... I should have done something. Should have stopped him. I ... Well, I'm just really sorry." Tam's eyes stung with tears as she held the knife out in her palm. "He would want you to have this back. I know it was special."

When she made no motion to get it, Tam leaned forward and dropped it in the woman's hand. Her face remained passive, but her fist closed around the object until her knuckles turned white.

Tam's body shook uncontrollably as she stared at the unmoving woman. Dover was all she had, and Tam had done this. She had allowed Dover to die. Tam wiped away her tears as Deena came back in the room.

"Thank you, but I have to be getting back."

Deena raised her eyebrows. "So soon?"

"Yes, sorry. My dad is waiting for me." Tam stood. "Goodbye, Mrs. Riggs."

She glanced back as she followed Deena into the kitchen. "Is she okay?"

Deena shrugged. "According to the medics, she's just in shock, but I'm not so sure. I haven't gotten her to eat anything since the news came. Come back and visit if you can. I think it's good for her. There was more color in her cheeks after talking with you just for that short time."

"I will," Tam promised.

As she turned to go, Deena touched her arm. "Thank you."

Tam nodded, but inwardly, she was wracked with guilt. Would Deena thank her if she'd known Tam had encouraged his recklessness? Would she smile if she knew it was because of her Mrs. Riggs had lost her only child? In that moment, she wished Mrs. Riggs had yelled at her. Wished she would have screamed, thrown her out, even hit her. Anything was better than seeing the shell of the woman Dover's mom had become.

With a heavy heart, Tam made her way back home.

Stopping when she got to the enclosure to wipe her eyes with her shirt, she looked for her father before letting herself in.

"Ah, about time. I thought you were going to sleep the day away." He thrust a net in her arms. "I need to check on a tear in cage three. Can you gather eight jays? We have an order to fill for the market today."

"Live?"

He grunted. "No one wants to see where the food comes from anymore. They'll need to be prepped too. Can you handle it?"

Tam was reluctant but nodded. "Yeah, I can handle it." She hated this part of the job. Holding the net firmly in her hands, she stared up at the flock of birds circling the enclosure. Jays didn't provide much meat. They were pretty bony, but they had an abundance of them, and they always seemed to be in high demand. Crossing the enclosure to the smokehouse, she opened the cabinet inside and pulled out a small blow gun, placed a dart in the end and took aim.

As soon as the dart struck, there would only be a few seconds to get the net under them before they fell. The birds were so carefree, darting this way and that. None of them suspecting they might be on a dinner table in a few short hours. She thought back to her friends. They had been so carefree before it happened too. Swinging and climbing through the forest. It was as close as she would ever get to flying. Dover didn't expect to be dinner for a bunch of kapros either.

A jay landed on a branch not too far from her. Tam aimed the dart at its chest. It turned its head and blinked at her a few times, curious what the Keeper was doing. Any moment it might fly away. Why did there have to be so much killing? She took a deep breath, preparing to blow into the tube. At least it would be over quickly for the bird. It wouldn't suffer like her friend.

CRASH.

The sound reverberated around her, making the blowgun fall to the floor, and the birds scatter. *What was that?* She squinted toward where the sound had come from. Nothing but a few leaves rustling in the distance. An earsplitting crack sounded, coming from the same direction. Tam slipped out of the enclosure and ran for the center of Aviary. The noise seemed to be coming from Raven district. As she ran, people around her came out of their homes, looking confused.

"What's going on, Tam?" Willow called as she joined her.

"I'm not sure, but I think it's this way."

After they reach the center of the village, they ran down the long bridge toward Raven.

"What were you doing in Sparrow district?" Tam asked as they went.

"I was looking for you. I just wanted some company, I guess. You and Hendrik ... Well, you're the only ones who know how I'm feeling, you know?"

"Yeah, I know what you mean." Another crash sounded as they passed several homes. This one was much closer.

Tam's eyes went wide. "Do you think it's the kapros?"

"I guess we'll find out soon enough."

As they came around a row of shops and passed by the scriptorium, they came to a screeching halt. The next bridge was broken. One half hung limply beneath them while the other was attached to a fallen tree. A large mound of upturned roots lay where the tree once stood. Other trees in the area were splintered and broken. An entire house was on the forest floor. Tam gasped. What if someone was in there when it fell? It didn't take long to figure out what caused the trees to fall. A sounder of kapros swarmed below with Pathfinders swinging back and forth, trying to keep them from ramming the trees again. A boar bashed into the tree in front of them. Tam pulled Willow aside just in time. The tree splinted the deck into pieces right where they had been standing.

"Get back!" a burly Pathfinder with dark curly hair commanded them.

"But we can help," Tam said.

Cassia dropped down next to them. "You heard him. Get back. This is a job for Pathfinders, not fledglings."

"But-"

"If you really want to help, you can start by evacuating Raven district."

"Is it really that bad?" Willow asked.

"We don't know, but we shouldn't wait until it is. Go, spread the word."

Willow nodded. "Come on, Tam."

Together, they raced back, banging on doors and shouting to everyone they saw to evacuate.

Mayor Steadman stepped out of one of the huts. "What's going on? Why are they clearing out the village?"

Tam pointed back toward where they had come. "The kapros. They're coming."

Chapter Thirteen

It was chaotic getting people to form orderly lines heading over the bridges. Panic was in their eyes. The kapros had never openly attacked Aviary. If they were no longer safe in the trees, where would they go? Tam raced back through the homes, making sure everyone was out. A young boy was walking around with a tear-stained face.

"My mom," he began as she approached.

"I'm sure she's with the others," Tam assured him. "Let's go find her." She held out her hand, but the boy refused to take it.

"No, she's not."

"Sure she is. Everyone left, see?"

"No, she's not," he insisted. The boy pointed toward the part of the village under siege. "Our house. She's in our house. It fell down, and I don't know how to get her back up."

The house Tam had seen. She had to make sure they knew someone was in there. "Willow!" she called.

Willow appeared around the side of a home. "What is it?"

Tam took the boy's hand and gave it to her friend. "Here. Take him out with the rest. I have to do something."

"Wait, why? You can't go back that way. You heard Cassia."

"I'll tell you later," Tam said over her shoulder as she ran back toward the wreckage. Arriving out of breath, she came to a stop at the edge of the splintered platform. Several more trees had fallen. The forest floor was littered with bloodied brown fur and the bodies of Pathfinders. Some of the bodies had been ripped apart. The other boars were desperately trying to get to them while the Pathfinders fought them back. Tam looked away, her stomach churning. She shook her head, remembering her mission.

She searched the trees and ground for Cassia, but her commander was nowhere in sight.

"Excuse me, sir?" she called to a man below, but he didn't seem to hear her. He was busy nocking another arrow in his bow. Everyone was too busy to notice her. Most of them fighting desperately for their lives. Tam spotted the house. It lay precariously beneath a huge tree that was barely being held up by the branches nearby. That wouldn't hold for long. Aside from being on the ground, it looked mostly intact. If only she'd brought her climbing gear.

Already regretting her decision, Tam grabbed on to a splintered plank and swung down to the backside of the nearest tree, hoping to stay hidden as she shimmied down to the ground. The leaves crunched as her feet touched the forest floor. She paused for a moment, taking a deep breath, then peered around the tree. It was only a few yards to the house. If she moved quickly, she might not draw notice amid the chaos. Tam counted down in her head.

Three ...

Two ...

One ...

She sprang from her hiding place, dodging a fallen limb and leaping over a dead kapros. The metallic smell of blood was everywhere. Without stopping, she leapt through an open window and rolled to the floor. The room was surprisingly quiet compared to the shouts and crashing just outside. A table and chair lay upside down against the wall and broken glass was strewn across the floor.

"Hello?" she called, getting to her feet. "Anyone in here?"

Tam walked to the next room, waiting for her eyes to adjust to the dim lighting. The glass crunched beneath her as she walked.

"Hello?" she called, looking through each room she came to.

As she was about to move on, a soft moan came from an overturned bed in the corner. Tam rushed over and saw a woman lying on her side, pinned behind the wooden frame, barely conscious. Blood dripped in her eyes from a gash on her head.

"My son," she whispered. "Where's my son?"

A crash shook the house. Tam flinched, remembering the tree overhead. "Your son is okay. I'll take you to him, but it's not safe here." Bending down, she heaved the bed up and off the small woman, dropping it with a clunk next to her.

"My leg ... I don't know if I can walk."

"I'll help you," Tam offered. Reaching for the woman's arm, she helped her stand. Together, they hobbled awkwardly across the room. Another crash made Tam look back. The light was streaming in through a large hole in the side of the wall, only obstructed by the furry silhouette of an angry kapros. Arrows stuck out of his blood matted fur. She remembered from her class that anytime a boar was injured without being killed, they became enraged.

Swallowing, Tam met the creature's black eyes for just an instant before it charged into the room. She whipped around the corner just in time. The beast smashed into the doorway behind them. Tam stumbled and hurried to help the woman back to her feet.

The boar collided into the door again. It could barely stand under the low ceiling, and it let out a snort of rage before running at them once more. Tam turned away, focusing all her energy on making it to the open window. They were moving too slow. At any moment, her back would feel the stabbing pain of those vicious tusks.

Chapter Fourteen

A creak followed by an ear shattering crunch filled the air. Tam didn't stop to see what it was. Something crashed into her side, sending Tam and the woman to the ground. She looked up just in time to see the wall they'd been racing toward fall outward to the ground. They were under the top of the large tree, but other than a few scratches, Tam felt okay.

"Are you alright?" she asked the woman.

She nodded, and together, they lifted the branches aside just enough for them to squirm out beneath them. The boar had been struck by the center of the tree. Even though it lay pinned under the heavy wood, it still dug its feet in the ground and struggled to get at them.

An arrow shot right into the kapros eye and caused it to go still. It was the archer Tam had seen before. He reached down and helped them to their feet. The fallen tree gave them a momentary peace from the battle, creating a makeshift wall.

Cassia appeared from over the top and leapt down. "Tam! What are you doing down here? I told you to stay back!"

"Sorry, but this lady was stuck in the house, and I—"

"Never mind." Cassia seemed to notice the woman for the first time. "Grant, help me get them out of here."

The man nodded and put his bow away. Reaching for his belt, he pulled out a grappling gun and shot it up to the platform above. Cassia did the same and instructed Tam to hold onto her back. Once Tam had a firm grip, the gun reeled in the rope, propelling them upward. They went up so fast, Tam gasped. I was exhilarating.

"Wow. When do I get one of those?" she asked, dropping down from Cassia's back.

"You *were* going to get them your third week," Cassia said with a frown.

Tam looked down and shuffled her feet. "Oh … right."

"Grant and I need to get back to the others. Can you help her from here?"

Tam put her arm around the older woman to support her. "Yes, we'll be okay." She turned to lead the woman back to the others.

"Oh, and Tam," Cassia said from the edge of the platform, "nice work." She gave a nod before disappearing back to the forest below.

After rejoining the others, they all gathered in the center of Aviary to wait. Hendrik pushed through the crowd and stopped next to Willow and Tam. "What's going on? I heard something about an attack?"

"Yes, in Raven district. It had to be evacuated," Willow said.

"What? That's crazy. Is everyone okay?"

"Well, Tam saw more than I did. She should have a better idea."

Tam blinked. "Hmmm?"

"Hendrik was asking if everyone is okay. What did it look like down there?"

Shaking her head, Tam muttered, "Not good. There were bodies on the ground. Lots of them. I-I don't know if they can stop them."

"Then why aren't we helping instead of standing here?" Hendrik asked. "Let's get our gear."

A hush fell over the crowd that had gathered. Tam followed their gaze and saw a group of Pathfinders walking toward them. Some of them were in bad shape and had to lean on the other ones for support. Tam sighed with relief to see Cassia among them.

"Medics, we need medics over here!" Cassia shouted. The crowd split to allow the medics to get through. While those with more serious wounds were taken away, the other Pathfinders talked quietly to the mayor and other village leaders.

"Has the attack stopped?" someone in the crowd shouted.

"When can we return home?" another asked.

Mayor Steadman held up his hands for quiet. "There is no need to panic. I have been informed the attacks have subsided. The Pathfinders were able to lead the kapros away. I will give you more details as I learn of them. For now, we must arrange temporary places to stay for those from Raven district. My assistant, Diana, will help organize and work out the details while I further confer with the Pathfinders."

The crowd grew noisy again, trying to get sleeping arrangements sorted out. Tam watched as the Pathfinders followed Steadman into a large meeting hut. She raised her eyebrows and inclined her head toward the hut.

"Shall we see what we can hear?" Tam asked.

"I don't know …" Hendrik said.

Willow rolled her eyes and pulled Hendrik along.

"Where are you guys going?" Grace blocked their path, her arms crossed.

Tam tried to push the other girl aside, but she didn't budge. "Move it. We don't have time to talk."

"You're going to eavesdrop, aren't you?"

"What are you going to do about it?" Tam scowled.

"Nothing, but I'm coming too." She turned and walked toward the hut.

Tam growled and followed after her. Pulling the curtain aside, they stepped in. A wall with a doorway on each side divided the entrance from the main room. They crept close to one of the doorways and listened. Tam inclined her head, trying to hear better.

"What is the situation, General Kaan?" It was the mayor who spoke. His voice sounded different when he wasn't addressing the village. Smaller somehow.

"My men have redirected them for now, but it's only a matter of time until the kapros return. It's what we feared. The food has grown so scarce, they're growing desperate. Now that they've discovered us, they will almost certainly be back and with greater numbers."

"W-what can be done? Do you have a suggestion?"

The mayor's question was met with a long pause.

Finally, the commander spoke up. "We have two options. We can fight, but they outnumber us by such an incredible number, it would just be prolonging our demise, or we can relocate."

"Relocate? But this is all we know. How can we survive without the gardens and the birds? Where will we go?"

"General?" Cassia spoke up now. "There are some caves to the east, but they aren't large enough to hold all of Aviary. Only two, possibly three, of the four districts would fit. Perhaps the strongest could stay behind and make a go of it here. We could send the young and the weak to the cave and-"

"No," Mayor Steadman cut in. "We'll need the strongest to help us survive."

"What are you saying?" Cassia's voice was steady, but there was a hint of anger in it.

"I'm saying, to survive we all must make sacrifices. The old, feeble, or sick will have to make sacrifices like the rest of us. That sacrifice will be staying behind for the good of all Aviary."

Tam swallowed, thinking of Gran. Would they really leave her behind? And Dover's mom. Would the mayor consider her among the weak in her current condition? She peeked around the corner in time to see Cassia step toward Steadman who took an involuntary step back.

Cassia's voice was low and fierce. "And exactly what sacrifice will *you* be making?"

General Kaan grabbed her arm and pulled her back. "Enough. We are here to inform and advise strategic action. Not to threaten."

The mayor straightened his coat. "We must do what we can for the greater good. In time, you'll see I'm right."

Tam's mind raced. There had to be a better solution. She felt her gran's notebook tucked inside her jacket. Maybe if they knew how this all began, they could put their head together to think of a possible solution. Opening the book, she removed the photograph and tucked it in her pocket. Without that, there was no way they could connect it to Gran.

"What are you doing?" Willow whispered.

But Tam was already stepping into the next room. She cleared her throat, and all eyes shot to her.

Steadman's eyes bulged. "What do you think you're doing in here? This is a private conversation." His face was a deep red.

Cassia's eyes flashed. "I'm sorry, Mayor Steadman. Tam, this is the third time today you've been where you don't belong. Go home."

"But I might have some information that could help."

Cassia grabbed her arm and started to pull her toward the door. Tam pulled free and slammed the book down in front of Steadman. "Just take a look at this. That's all I'm asking."

Cassia reached for her arm again, but the mayor held up his hand. Reaching down, he flipped through the first few pages, stopping at the image of the kapros. After a few moments, he sat back. A deep frown wrinkled his forehead. "Where did you find this?"

"I ... uh ..." She wracked her brain searching for a plausible answer.

"Because it's hilarious." Mayor Steadman let out a hearty laugh, making his stomach shake with merriment. "What an imagination this person has. If you wrote this Tam, you should consider being a storyteller at the next feast."

Tam's face burned with embarrassment. "I didn't make it up."

"Take a look at this, Commander." He turned the book so the others could get a good view. "Imagine, a magical serum that caused all this. Turned regular hogs into what? Super hogs?"

Sticking out her chest, Tam narrowed her eyes. "And why is that so hard to believe? Where do you think the kapros came from?"

"The deep jungle. We all know that. When humans disturbed their natural habitat, they turned on us."

Tam shook her head. "Why didn't they destroy the jungle they lived in? Why did meeting humans make them go berserk? Hogs given a serum makes just as much sense as that. More in fact."

"Enough. I don't have time to argue with a child. Take her out of here." He tossed the book back at her.

"But …" Tam objected. "If it was a serum, there could be a cure." Cassia and another Pathfinder grabbed her arms and pulled her toward the door. "If we just studied that book and tried to come up with an antidote or something, we might stand a chance!"

"That's enough," Cassia said as she pulled her outside. "You heard the mayor. Now get home where you belong."

"All right, all right. I'm going." Slumping her shoulders, Tam walked away, stopping at the next hut. When she turned back around, Cassia was going inside. Moments later, Willow, Hendrik, and Grace appeared from the meeting hut.

"Where did you guys go? I didn't see you in the entryway," she asked as they approached.

Willow stopped next to her. "We hid behind that big table, but let's not change the subject."

"Yeah, what is this book you're talking about?" Hendrik asked, taking it in his hands and turning it over.

"It's nothing it's just …" She stopped. The square was still bustling with noise, and she couldn't focus. "Come on," Tam said, leading them away from the chaos. A dining hall was open near the town center, so they ducked inside. After finding a quiet booth near the back, Tam pulled the notebook back out and showed it to them.

"Why didn't you show us this before?" Hendrik asked. He skimmed the pages with interest. "This could be huge."

Tam shrugged. "I just found it recently, and I didn't know if it was important or not."

Willow squinted at the sloppy handwriting, trying to make out some of the less legible parts. "How do you know it's real and not some tall tale like the mayor suggested?"

Tam glanced around to make sure no one was nearby before pulling the photo out of her pocket. "I found this inside. I'm pretty sure that young one is my great-grandma."

Grace snatched the photo away. "Your great-grandmother? You can't be serious. Why don't you ask her about the formula, you idiot? Maybe she knows a cure."

Shaking her head, sadly, Tam lowered her eyes. "Gran was injured in the old days. Hit her head pretty hard. She's never been all there since. Add that on top of the fact Gran's gotta be like a hundred, I don't think she'll be very helpful."

"Well, I don't know about the rest of you," Grace said, "but I'm going to go home and pack. You heard Mayor Steadman. All the able-bodied people are going to the caves."

Willow shook her head. "But Grace, you would leave so many behind? There has to be another solution."

Grace stood up. "That's not my problem. You'll change your mind, too, when the kapros come back. You'll see."

Willow slouched back in her chair as she watched Grace leave. A look of melancholy on her face. "Maybe we could at least try talking to your great-grandma."

Hendrik nodded. "Yeah, it can't hurt, right?"

Tam shrugged. "I suppose not. Alright. When do you want to come meet her?"

Hendrick stood up. "No time like the present, right?"

Chapter Fifteen

Tam knocked on the doorframe of Gran's room. "Can I come in? I brought some visitors."

"Visitors? How lovely!" Gran clapped her hands as they walked in. "You're just in time for sandwiches."

Tam sat on the edge of her great-grandma's bed. "These are my friends, Willow and Hendrik."

"Oh, how lovely, Mary. As long as visitors don't keep you from your duties."

Willow scratched her head. "Mary?"

Tam shrugged. "She gets a little confused. It's not Mary; it's Tam. Remember?"

Gran's eyes crinkled at the edges at the mention of Tam's name. "I have a granddaughter named Tam!"

"Quite the coincidence ..." Tam said with a nod and a smile.

Gran folded a napkin and handed it to Willow. "I hope you like cucumber sandwiches. That's all I have today. Mary needs to do the shopping." She rolled her eyes and shook her head in Tam's direction, then set to work putting together another sandwich out of a napkin.

"Listen, thanks for the sandwiches, Gran, but we really came to ask you a few questions." Tam placed the book in front of the old woman. "We need to know more about your work."

"Shhh, this is top secret! How did you get my notes?" She snatched up the book and held it to her chest.

"You gave it to me. Remember?"

"Oh." She let the notebook fall back to her lap.

Reaching down, Tam grasped the old woman's wrinkly hands in her own. "Gran, listen. The kapros are attacking Aviary. We need to know more about the experiments. Do they have any weaknesses? Is there a cure? An antidote?"

The old woman's eyes went wide. "The … the kapros are coming here?"

"Yes, that's why we need your help."

She jerked her hand away from Tam and covered her face. "No, no, it can't be. What have we done?" Letting out a hoarse scream, Gran flailed her arms, knocking the blankets to the ground. "Dead, everyone is dead. Blood, so much blood! I must go. I must escape this place."

"It's okay, it's okay." Tam placed her hand on the woman's arm. "You're going to be just fine. We're safe. We're in your room enjoying teatime, see?" She held up the napkin and pretended she was chewing. The old woman stopped thrashing, still heaving deep breaths. "That's it. See, we're all having a good time. I'd love another sandwich if you have one."

Gran smiled, and her breathing settled. "Of course! Just give me a few moments to get the ingredients back out."

As the old woman pulled out various cosmetics, setting them on her nightstand, Tam pulled her friends aside. "This isn't going to work. The subject is just too much for her."

Willow bit her lip. "But we can't give up already."

"You saw how upset she got. She's too fragile."

Hendrik leaned against the doorframe, deep in thought. "If only we could just get her to read the parts we can't decipher. It might give us some real insight."

"Hmm ..." Tam closed one eye. An idea was formulating. When she was a little girl, even with Gran's mental confusion, she was still able to read stories to her flawlessly. "I think I might know something that will work." Walking back to the bed, Tam sat next to Gran like she used to as a child. "Gran, can you read me a story?"

Reaching up, Gran touched Tam's cheek. Her face softened with recognition. "Tamerelda, when did you get here? Of course Grandma will read you a story."

Tam picked up the notebook, flipping to a page near the end with fairly legible handwriting. "Here, I want this one."

Picking up the book, Gran frowned for a moment. Tam scooted down on the bed, placing her head on the old woman's shoulder. The woman looked at her and smiled.

"Very well. This story is titled, 'April 4th.' An unusual title to be sure." She cleared her throat, then began. "My associates have been killed. The boars are everywhere and have surrounded the building. I have locked myself in the lab to find a cure. I hope my husband, Rob, is safe. I fear what kind of world our future children will face if I do not put an end to this here and now." Gran frowned. "This isn't much of a story. Still, it seems familiar."

Tam turned the page. "Go on. I want to see how the story ends," she encouraged her.

"April 12th. Heard on the news that boars are causing chaos in several cities. Everything depends on my efforts. Captured baby kapros in Room B. The room won't hold him for long. Have tried everything to reverse the condition to no avail. I continue to watch the boars interact from atop the lab. Even though they are highly aggressive and in a seemingly constant state of hunger, adult hogs do not attempt to devour each other. Could another dose cause them to turn on one another? Will test theory on captive kapros in the morning."

Gran turned to the next page, apparently now captivated. The next entry didn't have a date. She read the next couple of brief sentences. "Young hog got loose in the night. Lab is no longer safe. I escaped but hit my head. Bandaged it the best I could. Possible concussion? Going to find medical help and a place to wait this out with Diana. Will send others to retrieve the formula later."

"Diana?" Willow questioned.

"That's my grandmother's name," Tam explained. "She died when I was younger. She must have been just baby when they lived in Charleston."

The next page had only a few brief sentences. "Memory is blurry on the edges. Head injury likely culprit. Diana is my priority now. Found a group that will help keep us safe."

Gran closed the book. "And the princess and dragon lived happily ever after. My, what a riveting tale."

Tam nodded head. "Yes, thank you, Gran." She took the book from the woman's hands and gave it to Hendrik.

Leaning over, the old woman gave her forehead a kiss. "Now, off to bed. You don't want to stay up too late."

Tam stood and motioned for her friends to follow. "Goodnight, Gran."

"Goodnight, Tamerelda," Gran replied as they turned to leave. Once they were out the door, Tam led them to her room. They plopped down on her bed and sat quietly for a moment. Finally, Willow broke the silence. "So, how do we find the lab?"

"Are you serious?" Hendrick asked. "That's a suicide mission."

Tam stood up and began pacing, ignoring Hendrick's objections. "That's a great question, Willow. On the photo I found, it gives a name. Denton. I think Denton is the name of the lab, and I know my great-grandmother used to live in a town called Charleston. She used to tell me about it when I was young. Maybe the lab is there. I've seen a few old maps in my dad's room. I'll see if I can find them."

Tam opened her door and called for her father. When there was no response, she hurried to his room. Her dad had several old boxes in his closet. When she'd seen the maps before, he'd shooed her away. At the time, Tam thought he was a geography enthusiast or something and didn't want her to mess them up. Now, she wondered if they were left over from his days as a Pathfinder. It could be why he didn't want her to see them. The first box was full of nothing but old clothes. She shoved that one aside and looked at the next. It was full of old clothes, too, but after a little rummaging around, she found a stack of maps near the bottom of the box. "Bingo."

After carefully arranging the clothing back the way it was, Tam slid the boxes back into the closet and rejoined her friends.

"Found them," she announced and spread the maps out on the bed.

Hendrick looked over the maps thoughtfully, pulling on his bottom lip. Most of the maps were of the surrounding forest and had outposts and rivers marked out, as well as hazardous areas to stay away from. Helpful, but they weren't going to tell them how to find the lab.

Willow pulled out a map from underneath the others. "What did you say the name of that town was?"

"Charleston. Why? Did you find something?" Tam asked.

With a grin, Willow held out the creased paper. The map was old and yellowed. Probably made before the great wars. It was a printed map of the area with handwritten notations marking the location of Aviary within the surrounding area. Among the names, was a small, barely readable text just beyond the forest that showed the area of Charleston.

"It's closer than I thought," Tam said. She allowed a glimmer of hope to work its way into her chest. Maybe this wouldn't be such a difficult journey after all.

"Hold up," Hendrick said. "You can't mean for us to make this journey on our own?"

"If we don't, who will? No one believes us, and if we don't act, hundreds will die. Steadman plans to leave anyone he considers sick or weak behind as fodder for the kapros."

"Okay, let's say we make it and, by some miracle, find a serum that somehow survived all this time. Do you really want to risk giving it to the kapros on the off-chance that making them more aggressive and huge will help the situation?"

Tam sighed. "I know it sounds crazy, but what choice do we have?"

Shaking his head, Hendrick muttered something under his breath. "Okay then," he said. "I'll go. It's a stealth mission, right? Better if just I go, and you both head for the caves with the others."

Tam rolled her eyes. Typical, cocky Hendrick.

"There is no way we'd would let you go on your own," Willow spoke up.

Nodding, Tam agreed. "Yeah, get that out of your head. We're all going."

Hendrik narrowed his eyes and looked from one girl to the other. Finally, he sighed. "Fine then, but if we're going to do this, we're going to do it right. We need to be prepared and know what we're up against." He held up the other map he'd been studying of the forest. "This forest is bigger than it looks, and according to this map, we have to cross a large clearing before we reach the city."

Tam's heart sank. A large clearing would be a nightmare. With no trees to hide behind or climb, they would be completely vulnerable.

"But it is an old map," Willow chimed in. "Couldn't there be trees now?"

Hendrik shrugged. "It's possible, but we'll have to plan for the worst."

Willow stood up. "I agree, and we'll need more than our tree climbers. We need grapplers too."

"But where can we get those?" Tam asked. The thought of sneaking back into the camp and taking supplies out from under the other Pathfinder's noses didn't thrill her.

Willow smiled. "Lots of people in my family are Pathfinders, remember? Leave it to me."

Hendrik rolled up the maps. "All right then. While you're doing that, I'm going to study these maps and set a course for us to follow. Tam, can you gather some food for the trip?"

Tam nodded. She should be able to sneak some meat from the smokehouse without Dad noticing if she took just a small amount from each batch. "Sounds like a plan. Let's meet back here in exactly three hours."

"Right," Willow said. The three looked up at each other in silence, as if just in that moment feeling the full weight of their mission.

"We can do this," Tam said, but the crack in her voice betrayed her apprehension and made it sound more like a question.

Chapter Sixteen

"Do we have everything?" Hendrik asked. The three teammates stood at the southernmost part of Aviary. Each had on full gear and had spent the last thirty minutes practicing using the grappling system. They were far from proficient, but it would have to do for now.

"I have enough water to last us to the first river and enough food to last several days," Tam said.

"Good." Hendrik held out his fingers and counted them as if ticking off an invisible list in his head. "And we have gear for camping, the grapplers, our weapons, and a bag to bring back the serum."

Tam licked her lips. They were really doing this. In her mind, it would either end in triumph or complete disaster. She flexed her muscles, getting ready for the first jump.

"Ready?" Hendrik asked. Tam and Willow nodded. With Hendrik leading the way, they sprang from the platform. This time, even Willow didn't stray far from the group. After losing Dover, they all felt the unspoken need to stay close. Despite her feelings of apprehension and doubt about this mission, Tam still felt the same exhilaration as before as they jumped from tree to tree. The wind brought with it the smell of the fresh rain that had fallen that morning, mingling with the scent of the young sprouting leaves and bark. It was the smell of life.

She let herself fall into the rhythm. It was almost like a dance. Left, right, up, down. Always looking for the next jump or branch within reach. As they went along, Tam found her thoughts drifting to her mother. What would she think of all this? She knew what her father would think. He'd be so mad. Probably sure they would be killed. It was nice having him on her side for a short time. But now, coming home in disgrace, he had to be questioning the faith he'd put in her. Tam didn't blame him. She questioned it too. A trainee by a technicality, now kicked out of the Pathfinders and sent home. Could they really make a difference?

Tam glanced toward her companions. Hendrick was stony faced, and even Willow lacked the carefree nature she usually carried herself with. Dover was the best trainee that year by a mile, yet for all his strength and training, he'd been ripped apart in an instant by the kapros. Could they really hope to return alive, or were they rushing to their deaths?

Before she knew it, it was time to stop for a rest. Hendrik led them to an old outpost that was marked on the map. The structure was a bit rotten in places and missing a roof but overall solid. Tam leaned against the wall, not realizing how much her muscles ached until now.

Hendrik took a sip of water. "It's already getting dark. I think we should stay here for the night."

"But we don't have time to stop. We need to get that serum."

"He's right," Willow chimed in. "It's too dangerous to climb in the dark. We need to play it safe. Not take chances like … Well, we need to be careful."

Tam looked at the floor. She knew what Willow was about to say. Not like last time. "Yeah, okay. You're right, but we leave at first light." The high she'd gotten from jumping had worn off at the thought of Dover. If they'd had played it safe the first time, he'd still be alive. What were they even doing out here? Was this another mistake? Was Tam going to get them all killed this time? Looking down at the forest floor, she saw a hint of movement.

Hendrik put his hand on her arm. "It's not your fault."

Tam blinked. "What?" The gesture took her by surprise after his distance.

"Dover's death. It's no one's fault."

"I know. Deep down, I know, but I still feel guilty. I should have stopped him."

"There was no way you could have predicted what happened. And I could have tried harder to stop him too."

She looked at her hands. "I'm sorry for what I did. What I said. I was horrible."

"You were upset. We all were, but we're a unit. A team. We'll face whatever we have to together." Hendrik's deep brown eyes were full of sincerity.

"He's right." Willow agreed. "And Dover would want us to do this. For him and for his mom who's still alive and needs saving like the rest of the community."

Nodding, Tam found she believed them. Maybe things would be all right after all. "I visited her, you know. Dover's mom."

Willow's mouth formed an 'O'. "You did? What did she say? Did she seem all right?"

"She seemed ..." Tam searched for the right words. "Empty. Like nothing mattered anymore. The medic's say it's because of the shock. I promised to visit her again. If we get out of this alive, maybe you guys could join me."

"Absolutely. Right, Hendrick?"

But Hendrick was staring at the ground below. "Uh guys. I think we have company." He pointed down. The entire forest floor was moving. Tam squinted. No, it wasn't the ground moving. It was-

"Kapros," Hendrik whispered. "A huge sounder of kapros by the looks of it."

The trees shook and swayed as the hogs pushed their way clumsily through the forest. Several of them stopped and sniffed at the base of the trees holding the outpost. Tam swallowed. "Get away from the edge."

The three of them scooted toward the center of the platform, not wanting to take a chance of being spotted after seeing the desperation of the other kapros earlier. They couldn't really lift their necks, so the precaution was probably useless. It was more likely their hearing or sense of smell that might alert them to their presence. Tam glanced up. Maybe they should move higher while the kapros passed. Then again, that might make too much noise. She peeked over the edge again. Even more of the gigantic hogs had stopped to sniff the trees. They grunted and lifted their stubby heads as high as they could. Her mouth suddenly dry, Tam tried to take even, steady breaths.

"I think they can smell us," she mouthed to the others, then lifted her hands helplessly. Any moment, they might start crashing into the trees, trying to bring them down.

Hendrik picked up a branch and motioned for the girls to lean in close. "We need to get higher. I'll throw this as far as I can to distract them, then we climb."

Standing and stepping closer to the edge, Hendrik hauled his arm back, preparing to send the stick far into the distance.

Tam's eyes grew wide as she noticed the rotten board beneath where he stood. "Hendrik, wait!" But her warning didn't come soon enough. With a crack, the board splintered in two. Hendrik's foot plunged beneath the platform as the sound reverberated through the forest.

Tam and Willow rushed to help him up. "Are you okay?" Tam asked.

"I'm fine, but my leg is stuck."

Willow ventured a look over the edge. "Well, that did it. They know we're here now."

No sooner had the words left her mouth than the tree gave a hard jolt as one of the creatures crashed into it. The kapros were hungry, and they would do anything to get their next meal.

Another large crash shook the platform. Tam lurched forward. Willow grabbed her arm and helped steady her friend.

Hendrik still struggled to get his leg free. "Little help here, guys?"

Together, with one on each arm, the girls pulled with all their might, but he still didn't budge.

"I'll climb down and see if I can get it loose from that side," Willow offered. Another crash shook the trees.

Tam nodded. "Hurry."

Without wasting any time, Willow disappeared beneath them. "I see the problem."

Hendrik's face had gone pale. "Can you get it loose?"

"Maybe. I'm going to need you to twist your leg to the right. And Tam?"

"Yes, I'm here."

"Kick the board above his knee when I say it's ready."

CRASH

Tam reached for Hendrik's hand as the tree began to topple.

"Now!" came Willow's voice from below, where she'd miraculously managed to hold on. Grabbing Hendrik with one hand and the tilting tree with the other, Tam slammed her foot into the rotten wood. From there, it was all a blur. Tam lost her grip on Hendrik's hand as the tree fell. She leapt to a small nearby tree, barely managing to sink her claw into the bark.

"Hendrik!" she yelled as the tree crashed to the ground. Had he gotten free? The tree Tam clung to wasn't safe. It was teetering too. Quickly, she leapt to a bigger tree and then another, climbing higher with each one. The kapros seemed to have lost her scent for the moment. They continued their rampage on the trees surrounding what was once the outpost until they had formed a small clearing.

Only a few kapros remained now. Most had continued the stampede right where they left off as if they sensed something new to hunt. Tam made her way closer as the last of the boars joined their sounder. Afraid to call out in case it alerted more kapros or made the group return, she climbed down as fast as she could, searching the ground for any sign of Hendrik or Willow, but it was getting too dark to make out much.

Tam came across what was left of the outpost and prepared herself for the worst, but there was no sign of

Hendrik. She breathed a sigh of relief. If they'd attacked him, there would probably be a lot of blood. There was with Dover anyway. She reached out to lean on a nearby tree and pulled her hand back. The bark was damp and sticky. Tam looked at her fingertips in the moonlight and swallowed. It was blood.

Chapter Seventeen

After finding the blood on the tree, Tam was able to find several other spots on the trees nearby. Most of them were part way up, leading her to believe Hendrik was still well enough to climb. The trail of blood led her in the direction the kapros had gone. What was he thinking going that way? It was slow going finding the blood just by the light of the moon. Finally, she spotted something moving in the distance. Could it be Hendrik or Willow? Her hopes soared.

As Tam drew close, she saw it was only a female boar, separated from the group. It was digging and gnawing at something on the ground. The kapros was so intent, it didn't notice her presence. She climbed to a tree immediately overhead and strained her eyes to see what kept its attention so completely. Gasping, Tam nearly fell from her perch as she recognized Hendrik's green jacket. "No …" Her voice came out in a whisper as her eyes filled with tears of fear and rage. "No!" she screamed, dropping down on the animal from above with her blade drawn. The boar snorted and spun around as she landed on its back. With a cry of anger, Tam swung her blade down onto the back of the animal's neck with all her might. To her shock, the blade cut the kapros's head completely off. She ducked into a roll as the limp, headless body fell to the ground.

Dropping her blade, Tam stared at her hands as the blood from the creature soaked the leaves around her. Not even Dover had been able to do what she had done. Remembering Hendrik, she dropped to her knees and scooped up his jacket. I was badly shredded and covered in sticky red blood. This was all that was left of her friend. And he had been her friend all along. Him and his stupid, arrogant, wonderful face. His dimples, his dark eyes. She would never see them again. Tam held the jacket close, not caring if she got blood on her face.

Tam needed to get back to the trees, but at that moment, she just didn't care. A sob shook her body as she rocked on her knees. There was a rustle in the forest behind her, but she didn't move. They'd taken so much. Let them take her too.

"Tam, are you okay?" It was Willow's voice. Tam turned, relieved to know Willow was okay. But how could she break the news to her? It was Tam's idea to go on this ridiculous mission, and now, she'd gotten someone else killed.

With a shaking hand, she held up the jacket. A dark shape loomed behind Willow. *No, not another kapros!* Tam opened her mouth to warn her friend, but before she could say a word, Hendrik stepped into the moonlight. "Oh, you found my coat. Or what's left of it anyway." He reached forward and fingered the torn cloth. "What happened here? Are you alright? Did you do this?" He motioned toward the dead kapros.

Tam's emotions swirled. Relief, confusion, fear. "Hendrik ... I-I thought ..."

"You thought what?" He dropped the jacked. "Ugh, it's covered in kapros blood." He looked from Tam's tearstained face to the bloodied boar. His face changed from a look of concern to a look of realization. "Did you think I was dead? Is that why you're upset?" His lips twitched at the corner.

Tam wanted to slap his smug face again. Here she was worried out of her mind, mourning his death, and he was smiling like an idiot. "Oh, grow up." She picked up the bloodied coat and threw it at him.

"Hey!" Hendrik knocked the coat aside with a grin. He took a look at the dead beast, seeming to notice it for the first time. His eyes went wide. "How in Aviary did you manage to hack the head clean off?" Before she could answer, a twig snapped nearby, bringing them to their senses.

"Let's get back to the trees," Willow urged as she pulled herself onto a branch. The other two wasted no time climbing up after her.

"So, what was with all that blood on the trees?" Tam asked Willow as they looked for a good spot to set up their hammocks. "I thought it was Hendrik's."

"Oh, it was. He purposely rubbed it on the trees to lead the Kapros away from us with his scent. He didn't know where we were, or if we'd fallen, so he said it was the only thing he could think of to keep us safe. I only found him a few minutes before you."

"Oh," was all Tam could think to say. It hadn't occurred to her that he might be leading them away on purpose. No wonder the kapros had suddenly stampeded away.

That night, they spent the next few hours getting what little sleep they could in hammocks stretched across the trees. Once the morning dawned, they set off to fill their canteens at the stream. Thanks to the run-in with the kapros, they were making good time and getting close to the clearing.

Being so exposed over a long stretch like that made Tam nervous. It was the part of the journey she'd been dreading the most. Up ahead, Hendrik came to a stop. Tam and Willow landed next to him. After a morning of travel, they'd arrived. The clearing sprawled out in front of them. Tall patches of grass dotted the landscape with the nearest trees being only small saplings that wouldn't even hold Willow's weight.

"According to the map, this used to be a large highway," Hendrik said.

Willow wrinkled her nose. "What's a highway?"

"You know, a place where cars used to drive. Haven't you seen them in the history books?"

History books were what they called all the literature and magazines that the Pathfinders would sometimes bring back after a hunting mission. Tam had always found them fascinating.

Willow shrugged. "Yeah, I guess so. Never paid too much attention.

Tam couldn't believe it. "Wow, a highway!" she exclaimed. I remember reading about these. And those things on wheels that use to go on them. Cars, right? I'll bet we'll even see one in the town."

"Yeah," Hendrik said. "I'm sure we'll see quite a few. Cars were the main way people used to get around. In fact, I think I see one down there now."

Tam looked around excitedly. There under a clump of weeds was a rusty metal frame with broken windows. "Whoa, that's so cool! Let's go check it out."

Hendrik held his hand in front of her. "Unfortunately, we also have company."

Several kapros were sprawled across the road. Tam hadn't noticed them before because they were laying down, blending into the dirt and leaves. "You think they're dead?"

"Looks more like they're sleeping," Willow said. "How will we get past them? Once they catch a whiff of us, won't they wake up?"

Tam looked down at the forest floor. "Not necessarily."

"What do you mean?" Willow asked.

"Well, maybe there is a way to cover our scent. Some way to smell natural and as close to the environment as possible."

Hendrik pointed to a pile of boar dung. "Not much more natural that that." He winked.

Willow's eyes grew wide. "No. Way."

"I was thinking more along the lines of dirt and leaves," Tam said with a grimace. "But by all means, Hendrik, feel free to use the dung. Not that it would change your scent much." She winked back at him before climbing down to the ground.

"Ha, ha. Such a comedian all of a sudden." Hendrik landed softly next to her, followed by Willow. Reaching down, Tam grabbed a fistful of dirt and began rubbing it all over her body. The others followed suit, even shoving leaves in their shirts and pants. Pretty soon, they looked like some unearthly dirt monsters.

"Missed a spot," Hendrik said and threw a fistful of dirt at Tam's head.

Tam sputtered and spat. "Hey," she whispered, grabbing a clump of dirt and smearing it in his face.

"Shhh, guys," Willow urged. "Don't forget, we're trying to *not* wake the kapros, not invite them to lunch."

Hendrik and Tam both looked at each other and grinned before showering Willow with leaves and dirt.

"Ha, jokes on you," she said, standing up and trying not to cough. "Now I'll be safer than either of you."

A snort made Tam jump. "Willow, shhh."

"Now you're shushing me?"

"Yeah, I heard something. One of them might be waking up." She peered through the leaves, but they were all still asleep. Breathing a sigh of relief, she motioned for the others to join her.

"I mapped out a route in my head that keeps up the farthest from them," Hendrik whispered. "Follow me."

He took a step out into the clearing, keeping low with his blade drawn. Willow nocked and arrow in her bow before going after him. Following suit, Tam unsheathed her shoka and held it out. She was surprised by the firmness of the ground underneath her. Was it made of wood? Reaching down, she felt the cool, smooth ground. I seemed to be made out of dark, rock-like material. How did they form the rock so perfectly flat for the highway? Must have taken years.

Willow tapped on her shoulder and nodded in Hendrik's direction. Right, she needed to stay focused. Keeping her knees bent, Tam walked along, trying to avoid twigs and branches. They were passing by the first kapros now. Its back was turned to them, and so close Tam could see the individual hair follicles. Its enormous bulk went up and down with each breath, like a hairy breathing mountain. It smelled like a mixture of feces and rotten eggs. She held her own breath while passing by. Both because of the stench and because she didn't trust herself to breathe quietly enough.

They passed another one. It was slow and painstaking, but the dirt and leaves seemed to be doing the trick. They only had to go between two kapros now, and then they were home free. As they climbed over the stone barrier in the center, Tam's foot slipped. She cringed at the grinding sound it made and quickly spun around to make sure none of the creatures had woken. The biggest one up ahead that they still needed to pass by stirred, rolled over, and was still. Tam let out the breath she'd been holding with a quiet whoosh.

Hendrik was passing between the two kapros now. The larger of the two was facing them, his tongue hanging out as he slept. As Tam went by, he exhaled, and the warm, sticky heat blew across her arm. She shivered, looking at the bits of meat stuck between his teeth, remembering how quickly the boar's teeth ripped Dover to pieces. A twig snapped ahead of her.

Willow froze with her foot on the branch, her mouth hanging open. Tam turned and saw the beast next to her staring back with gleaming, hungry eyes.

Chapter Eighteen

Tam jumped back, hitting something warm and bristly. She whirled around to see the other boar standing behind her. Instinctively, she flailed her blade out. It bounced harmlessly off the boar's hard skin and clattered to the ground. The beast lunged at her with a squeal of excitement, mouth wide. Its mouth was over her shoulder in an instant, but the pain didn't come. She opened her eyes to see it flailing around with an arrow through its cornea. Blood gushed from the fresh wound. Willow nocked another arrow and shot it point blank in the other eye.

Hendrick was hanging onto the bigger boar by the fur and trying to climb on its back. The two went around and around as the kapros tried to sink his teeth into him. Tam shook herself, adrenaline pulsing through her veins. Picking up her blade for a moment she froze, recalling Dover's last moments, but Hendrick needed help. Limbs heavy with dread, she took one step, then another, willing her body to move despite her rapidly beating heart. The boar spotted Tam and quit trying to bite Hendrik so it could go after her. It ran toward her, giving no heed to the other human scaling his back. She dodged to the side at the last minute and went into a roll. The thing turned in an instant, barely giving her time to stand. Jamming the back of her blade into the ground she jumped out of the way again. It stuck into its target, but the wound was only deep enough to make it go into a rage. Double speed, it flipped around and grabbed Tam's backpack. She gasped as she was lifted off her feet. The animal whipped its head around. Her scream echoed off the trees as her body slammed into the ground. Through an ever-darkening world, Tam saw Hendrik over the creature's shoulder. He brought his blade down on the boar's neck, but it kept going, bucking Hendrik off and running toward Willow with Tam's pack still between its teeth.

Tam's blade was stuck beneath the kapros's arm. Reaching up, with the last of her strength, Tam hit the butt of the blade as hard as she could right before the world went black.

She woke to find Willow and Hendrik crouched over her. "What happened? Where are we?"

"You killed it!" Willow exclaimed. "And it turns out, that the kapros will eat their own kind if they're already dead.

They were distracted enough by the two bodies that we were able to get you out of there and under this bridge. Hendrik says it's called an overpass."

Hendrik lifted her arm gingerly and examined it. "How are you feeling?"

Looking at the scratches on her body made Tam's stomach churn. A deep gash on her arm was the most painful. She felt around the cuts and bruises. "It hurts like crazy, but I don't think anything's broken."

She'd been fortunate. If that boar had clamped down on her back instead, she'd have more than some bumps and gashes.

Hendrik took off his shirt and tore a strip of fabric from it. Wow, he was ripped. Tam looked away before he could notice her staring.

Willow caught her gaze and raised her eyebrows. "I'm going to, uh … I'm going to scout ahead a little. Be right back." She shot Tam a knowing look before disappearing from under the archway.

Rolling her eyes, Tam held her arm out and allowed him to wrap it up. When he was done, he gave her arm a soft kiss. His cheeks immediately flushed a dark crimson red. "Sorry. I'm used to bandaging up my kid sister when she gets hurt."

Tam couldn't remember seeing him embarrassed before. She grinned, relishing the moment. "*Surrre*. I know you've been dying to kiss my arm ever since the first day we met. I don't blame you. It *is* an attractive arm after all."

A sheepish smile spread across Hendrik's face. "Don't flatter yourself. I've seen better." He winked and released her arm.

Tilting her head, Tam wondered why she'd never known Hendrik had any siblings. She'd never really thought about his family life before. "I didn't know you had a sister."

"I have five actually."

"Wow. All younger?"

He laughed, his eyes crinkling at the edges. "Yeah, I'm outnumbered. Hope I can make them all proud."

"I'm sure you will. How old are they?"

"They're all pretty young. Hettie is the oldest. She's eleven. I plan to teach her tree jumping next year." Hendrik's smile suddenly disappeared.

"What's wrong? Did you hear something?"

"No, I … I just realized something. Most of them are probably too young to go to the caves. If we fail …"

Tam put her hand on Hendrik's bare shoulder. "We won't."

Willow appeared back under the arch. "Guys, the streets are pretty deserted right now. I think it's a good time to move." She looked from Hendrik to Tam. "What happened? Am I missing something?"

Hendrik stood, pulling his torn shirt back over his head. "No, let's go. We don't have any time to waste."

Willow grabbed her pack, followed him down the hill, then looked back over her shoulder. "You coming?"

"Yeah, I'll be right there." Tam's heart hadn't stopped pounding since Hendrik had taken off his stupid shirt. She had more important things to think about, but it was a difficult image to shake. Pausing, she touched her arm where his lips had been moments before, then grabbed her gear and followed the others.

Walking down the empty street seemed so surreal. The homes and buildings had vines growing over them, and long, wild grass peeked up from every crack in the dark, rocky ground. It was so strange to think people used to live like this. Didn't they miss the trees? How did they ever feel safe with all this open space? Of course, there was a time they didn't need the shelter of the trees to protect them from the overgrown beasts that now inhabited the world. What would that be like? As they went along, they tried not to stay in the open for any longer than they had to, ducking into doorways and behind bushes every chance they could.

After a while, Tam started noticing signs on posts. One of them had the letter 'H' on it and said hospital beneath it in bold letters. It had an arrow pointing to the right. She was pretty sure they had labs inside of hospitals. In a small town like this, they probably didn't have too many different medical facilities.

"Guys," she whispered. "I think we should follow that sign. It could lead to a hospital with a laboratory."

They agreed, and Tam took the lead for a while, following the 'H' signs and turning each time toward the arrows.

Finally, they came to several huge buildings. Tam had no idea they could get that big. She stopped behind an overgrown car and scanned the area. Several kapros went in and out of the alleyways around the building straight ahead. The faded sign said it had been something called a bowling alley. Whatever that was. If they went around it on either side, they would be spotted.

"Should we go through the building?" she asked.

"Seems like the best way," Hendrick said. "Maybe there is a door leading out the back."

They waited patiently for the kapros to turn away, then snuck closer and dashed between two large green containers overflowing with trash. Willow reached the door first.

"Locked," Tam said with dismay. Another set of doors was to the right. One of the lower glass panes had been broken and pointed it out to the others. "There," she whispered.

They rushed over to the doorway and slid one at a time on their bellies, being careful not to cut themselves on the glass. "Hurry," Tam hissed. The snout of a boar was just coming around the corner when Hendrick's feet disappeared inside. Tam threw herself through the opening, wincing as a piece of glass sliced her back on the way in. She scrambled away from the door, not wanting the kapros to pick up her scent. Tripping over something behind her, she gasped and fell to the floor. Her heart pounded, waiting to see if any kapros had heard.

After a few moments, she let out a sigh of relief. "That was a close one, eh, guys?" No one responded. They just stared down at her, mouths agape. "Guys? What is it?" Something was touching her shoulder. Glancing sideways, Tam saw an eerie grin and jumped to her feet, shoving it aside. Her eyes went wide with horror when she realized she had been laying on a pile of bodies. Nothing was left but bone, hair, and tattered clothes. A scream began to escape her throat when Hendrick clamped his hand firmly over her mouth.

"Shhhh, it's okay. Quiet, remember? We need to be quiet." He removed his hand, and she took a few rasping breaths and closed her eyes. *Breathe, just breathe*, she told herself.

Willow knelt and examined the remains. "Looks like a family died here. Probably while hiding from the kapros."

Tam brushed off her clothes and shivered, staring at the little group of skeletons. Three larger ones, one mid-sized, and a small one. Tam was struck with a wave of sadness for this family when she realized the smaller skeleton must have been a child. To distract herself, she turned away and glanced around the rest of the large room. Rows of wood planks stretched across to the other side. She squinted in the dim lighting. Some sort of white statues stood at the end of the rows. How odd.

"We should keep moving," she murmured. "This place gives me the creeps."

They headed toward the doors on the far side when a crash made Tam spin back around. It had come from the far end of the wooden floor near the statues. Backing away, her eyes darted back and forth. Had a kapros gotten in through the back? Her muscles tensed, ready to run.

Another crash had Tam and her friends scurrying back, exchanging nervous glances. A look back from where they'd come in showed that still wasn't an option. The kapros still rooted around just outside. The only other door in the room was in the direction the sound had come from.

"Should we check it out?" Hendrik asked.

"I don't think we have much of a choice," Tam said, pulling her shoka from its sheath.

Willow and Hendrik followed, holding their blades in front of them.

"Ladies first," Tam said, motioning for Hendrik to go on ahead.

With a nod, he dismissed her remark and crouched low, stepping forward. Tam and Willow were close on his heels. So close that Tam bumped into Hendrik when he stopped with his hand on the door.

"Sorry."

"Shhh." Hendrik shushed her, waving his hand impatiently. He wiped a bead of sweat from his forehead before pushing the swinging door open a crack.

"I don't see anything," he whispered and pushed the door open a little wider. Tam let her muscles relax. Maybe it was nothing. The wind blowing in from a window knocking something over or a stray bird. She peered over Hendrik's shoulder into the back room. Dark except for the light filtering in through the crack. A motion near the floor caught her eye. A brown mouse? No. A shoe. A lone shoe. But it wasn't alone. She gasped, following it upward and saw the face of a man rushing toward them on all fours, galloping like a horse. With torn clothes, spittle on his chin and eyes wide with feral energy, he approached, ramming the door with his shoulder and sending them sprawling.

Chapter Nineteen

Tam tried to stand, but the man stood with his foot planted firmly on her chest. A man? How could this be? They were the only humans left, weren't they? She stared up at the man's face. A wild beard covered his chin, and his hair was matted and full of pine needles and moss. Though he had dark circles under his eyes, they were bright, alert, and gleaming with ferocity. He held a spear above his head, poised and ready to bring it down on her. He laughed with glee, showing a row of half rotten, brown teeth. "I'll get ya, little piggy! *Eee hee hee.* I'll be having bacon tonight!" His voice was raspy and had a singsong quality. She grasped around, searching for her shoka, but it had flown out of reach.

"Drop it!" Willow yelled from a few feet away. Her bow was nocked with an arrow and drawn back to her cheek.

"Please, no," Tam said, putting her hands in front of her face.

The man hesitated, furrowing his brow. "The piggy speaks?" He glared at Tam. "Tricks!" he shouted. Spittle flew from his mouth as he raised the spear again. Hendrik crashed into the man, tackling him to the ground. With a burst of incredible strength, the man easily threw Hendrik aside. Hendrik's head hit the wall with a thud, and he fell to the floor, unmoving.

Willow's bow wavered, unsure of what to do as the man came at her next. Tam grabbed his arm. "Stop, please!" she urged. "We mean you no harm." The man tore his arm away and spun back toward Tam, retreating a step.

Willow lowered her bow and held out her hands. "That's right. We won't hurt you."

He took another step back, and another, his eyes wide with fear. "Tricks ... Tricks! Piggies cannot speak!"

"We're human, like you." Tam spoke in a low, gentle voice. "I'm Tam, and that's Willow and Hendrik."

"Nooo!" Shoving his hands over his ears, the man hunched over and loped back through the doorway.

Tam rushed over to Hendrik. He was still breathing. A low moan escaped his lips as Willow and Tam helped him sit up. Blood dripped from a wound in his forehead, and a large goose egg was already forming. Pulling off her pack, Tam searched for something clean to stop the bleeding. A box slid toward her across the floor.

"A first aid kit!" She glanced up to see the man peering through the door. "Thanks." The man grunted and disappeared again.

"Are you okay?" she asked Hendrik while digging through the supplies and pulling out some gauze.

"Yeah, fine," Hendrik mumbled. "But man, what a headache."

As she dressed Hendrik's wound, Tam's eyes kept darting to the door, but the man didn't re-appear.

"How is this possible? Another human? I wonder how he survived and where he came from."

Willow shrugged. "I don't know, but he seems even more confused than we are. I wonder if he's been on his own all this time."

"Well he had to come from somewhere. He couldn't have just sprouted from the ground. Maybe there is another village out there. There could be more tree dwellers or even people surviving in the city!"

"No." The voice came from the doorway. "No more. Jacob be all there is left." The man crept out and sat cross-legged a few feet away, tilting his head and staring at them with interest. Hendrik jumped and started to stand. Tam and Willow placed their hands on his shoulders and held him in place.

"It's okay," Tam assured him. "I don't think he's going to hurt us."

His clothes hung from his lean muscular body in tatters, and his shoes were worn and had large holes in them.

"I'm Tam," she said, pointing and introducing herself again. "You said your name is Jacob?"

The man put his hand on his chest. "Yes, I be Jacob, the king of this city. The piggies be me only subjects." He threw his head back and let out a rueful laugh. "King Jacob of the Land of Swine."

"And you're really all alone, Jacob?" Willow asked.

Jacob nodded. "Alone. But it not be so bad. I makes the rules, and Jacob can sleep in as long as he likes." At this, he launched into another fit of laughter.

"Where did you come from, Jacob? Where are your people? Do you know somewhere safe?"

"My people?" Jacob stroked his ragged beard, and a far-off look came over him. "Years ago came from a cave. The piggies ... the piggies kill all but me. But Jacob be fast, and Jacob be smart." He tapped a long-nailed finger to his head. "Yes, I be too smart for them. I became king, you see. King of the world."

Tam's shoulders slumped. I guess there wasn't any other village. They were alone after all. Yet here was Jacob. How had he survived on his own for so long?

Hendrik winced and shifted. "Jacob. Maybe you can help us. We're looking for a lab."

Jacob grunted. "Lab?" He scratched his head.

"Yes," Tam chimed in. "Do you know of a laboratory anywhere? It would have lots of glass tubes, desks, maybe papers and files. It might be at a hospital or other large facility."

The man frowned. "Don't ... don't know. Must go tend to my affairs. It's tea time at the castle." Abruptly, the man stood.

"Wait," Tam called after him, but he was already going through the door. It swung shut behind him with a bang. She sighed. "Well, it was worth a shot."

The door swung back open. Jacob squinted at them. "Do you wish to visit the castle?"

"Uh ..." Tam scratched her head and glanced at her friends. Hendrik scrunched up his face. "We don't really have time to-"

"Absolutely! We want to visit the castle!" Willow said, nodding enthusiastically.

"Come," was all he said before disappearing again.

Willow and Tam helped Hendrik to his feet. He winced.

"Are you going to be okay?" Willow asked.

Hendrik nodded. "Yeah, I think so. Guys, we really need to keep looking for the lab. All of Aviary is depending on us. We don't have time for this."

"I still think this guy knows something," Tam said. "Finding the lab by ourselves might take days. Isn't it worth it to spend a few minutes to find out if he can help?"

Hendrik sighed. "I guess so, but we need to be on guard. He could be dangerous. He seems off. You sure we should trust him?"

"Any better options?" Tam asked and went out the door before Hendrik could respond. Hendrik sighed and followed her. Jacob was fast. They had to run to keep up with him some of the time, and other times, he would come to a halt, scanning the area before moving forward again. He led them down alleyways and through buildings. They finally made their way up a fire escape to the rooftops. Here, they were able to move quickly without fear of running into kapros. Crude bridges were built between the buildings, so they only had to leap in a few places. It was much like their village in the trees, and Tam felt almost at home as they sped along. How wonderful it felt to be up high again with only the sky above. But it didn't last long. As they came to the edge of one of the buildings, she sucked in her breath. The buildings here were in ruins.

"What happened here?" she asked.

Jacob waved dismissively. "Ah … the royal subjects be a bit excitable at times. They smash and crash," Jacob said. "Me kingdom may not be here much longer. But I be smart. When they find me, I move to a new castle. Come. We're almost there!"

Up ahead, they came to some scaffolding atop a mini mart. It stretched up precariously. Boards lashed and nailed together all around the main structure, with a shorter structure on each side. It did almost look like a castle. And situated atop it all was something yellow. Bright yellow tubing of some kind with flags flowing off the towers. They leapt across onto a platform on the right side of the scaffolding.

They climbed up a ladder to a platform and then another ladder, scaling upward until they came to the top of the structure. "Playtime Bouncy Castle," she read aloud. It was written on the side of the yellow tubing. Tape was wrapped around each corner and in several patches along the front.

"My royal chamber," Jacob said with a bow before plopping down on an overstuffed love seat in front of the yellow castle. "I sleep on air. It be very comfy. Very comfy indeed." He laughed and motioned for the others to pull up a chair. "Come. Approach the throne! It's been too long since I've entertained guests."

Tam pulled up a wooden barrel and sat down.

Jacob suddenly jumped up, snapping his fingers. "Where are me manners? Let me offer you some tea." He stooped down and started a fire in a small stove, placing a kettle on top.

Tam glanced around. A large doll with staring blue eyes sat in a chair to the left of Jacob's throne, and a pumpkin with eyes of coal and a carved mouth sat on his left atop a spike with a man's jacket across the shoulders.

"I see you're getting acquainted with my friends." Jacob said with a grin. "Let me introduce you. This pretty young lady is Pricilla." He motioned to the doll. "No, I'm not forgetting you," he said to the pumpkin. "And this jaunty fellow is Pumpkin Jack."

Willow swallowed. "I, uh … I thought you said you lived alone."

Jacob let out a roaring laugh. "They don't be real, you silly girl. They just keep me company."

"Oh." Willow let out a sigh of relief.

Jacob tilted his head. "What's that, Pricilla? No, no. I just have to say that so we don't scare our new friends. Yes, yes. Of course you're very real, indeed." Turning back to Tam, Willow, and Hendrick he put his finger to his lips. "*Shhh*, she's very sensitive about being a doll." He rolled his eyes. "Women."

Tam let out a nervous laugh. "You sure have a nice place here."

Jacob poured the tea and handed them each a chipped cup. "Why, thank you. I decorated meself."

Hendrik set his tea aside. "We really don't have time to stay long. We need to know if you've heard of the lab we're looking for."

Jacob wrinkled his nose. "No, I still don't know of any lab. No way, no how. More tea?"

"It's called Denton," Tam chimed in. "Does that sound familiar?"

Jacob stopped, his hand on the kettle. "Den-ton. Hmm …"

Tam leaned forward. "Then you've heard of it? You've heard of Denton Laboratories?"

"No."

"Oh, that's too bad." Tam's shoulders fell.

"There be a school called Denton though. Does that help?"

Willow clapped her hands together. "A school? They might have a lab at a school. I've read about colleges having things like that."

Hendrik stood. "Then what are we waiting for. Can you take us there, Jacob?"

"Will you excuse us for a moment?" He motioned toward his lifeless companions.

"Uh, sure ..." Hendrik said. They walked a few steps away. Jacob turned and whispered into the doll's ear, then into the pumpkin's. He waited as if listening, then laughed and slapped the pumpkin man on the back. The head fell off, and he quickly stooped down, brushed it off, and replaced it. Finally, he joined the others. "Aye, I can take you. Pricilla is being difficult, but she'll be getting over it soon enough. Come. It's not far." He motioned for them to follow, then ran on all fours to the ladder. Tam waved to the doll and the pumpkin, then blushed when she saw Hendrik watching. He smiled and gave them a wave as well.

After following Jacob down the scaffolding and through a couple of buildings, they climbed down and came to a stop at the edge of a large, grassy area. Jacob crouched low behind some bushes and pointed across the lawn. Tam peeked over the bush and read aloud. "Denton College. It is a school!" she whispered with excitement. "This must be it."

"Thank you, Jacob," Tam turned toward the man, but he was gone.

"Wow. I didn't even see which way he went," Willow said.

Hendrik nodded. "Sure was lucky we found him though. This would have taken forever to find."

"Now what?" Tam wondered aloud. "Not much cover ahead and so many buildings."

"I think I see a map." Willow pointed to a square sign ahead. "Maybe that will tell us something. I'll go. You guys wait here and keep a lookout." Before either of them could object, Willow darted forward, running straight for the sign.

Hendrik gasped. "She should have waited until we made sure the coast was clear!" He stood and quickly scanned the area. Tam went to the other side of the bush and searched the tall grass for signs of movement.

"All clear on my side," Hendrik said. "How does it look over there?"

Tam was about to give the all clear when she saw the grass swaying. A large brown snout emerged, sniffing the air. It was only about a man's height away from where Willow stood. The sign was the only thing that kept it from instantly spotting her friend. Willow was oblivious to the kapros's presence, but she wouldn't be for long. It had obviously caught her scent. It sniffed furiously. A loud grunt made Willow freeze.

"No, no, no ..." Hendrik said under his breath. "It's right on top of her, and there's nothing but open field around. Nothing to climb."

The boar took a step forward. Any moment, it would spot Willow. Tam spotted a car down the road. Maybe she could shoot it with an arrow and make a clang to distract it. Did she have time? Tam grabbed her bow and fumbled for an arrow. No, it was too late. The boar was inches from the sign.

A loud whistle broke the silence. It came from the top of a building near the car.

"Jacob!" Hendrik said with a grin.

Jacob stood with his fingers in his mouth and gave another whistle. The grass rustled all around and nearly a dozen hidden kapros raced from the grass toward the sound.

"Now's our chance," Tam whispered. Grabbing Hendrik's hand and pulling him along, she raced by Willow, motioning her to follow, and they sped toward the first building. The first door was locked. They ran alongside until they came to a shattered window and leapt inside. Vines had made themselves inside the building and up the inside of the walls. A small tree grew under a skylight in the lobby. They made their way further inside, away from the open windows and out of sight.

"Did you get a good look at the map?" Tam asked when they had all caught their breath.

Willow nodded. "I think so. I saw a building that was labeled 'Research Facility'. That sounds right, doesn't it?"

Tam's eyes lit up. "Yes, great job! Where was it?"

"Just a couple of buildings away. Come on. Let's see if there's a back way out of here."

They made their way through the hallway and out a back window. From there, they crept forward, darting from one building to another. Up ahead, they saw a red brick building.

"Denton Research Lab," Tam read aloud. It was written in black letters across the top of the building. "Bingo." They came to a set of large glass doors at the main entrance. Hendrik pried them open with his blade, and they stepped inside.

"How will we find the serum in such a big place?" Willow asked.

Stopping in front of a white sign, Tam ran her finger down the list of departments. Laboratory for genetic modification. Room 212. That sounded promising. Tam led the way up the stairs, through the deserted, eerie building. Wallpaper was peeling from the walls, and the cabinets and molding were caked with a layer of thick dust. Hendrik sneezed from behind her.

"Bless you!" Willow chirped.

Up ahead, Tam saw the numbers 212 on a wooden door. The door stood slightly ajar. "Well, this was a lot easier to find than I thought. We should be back home in no time." As she swung the door open, her face fell. Hundreds of vials covered the shelves that lined the entire room.

She stepped inside, making room for the others to enter. Hendrik gave a low whistle. "Wow."

Tam took in the rest of the room. Several stations were set up with paper and various vials and droppers laid out. She stopped when she came to a desk with a photograph of Gran as a young woman standing next to an attractive man. "Gramps," she whispered, running her fingers over the man in the image. Gramps had died nearly ten years ago. She'd almost forgotten what he looked like. Tam slipped the photograph in her bag and turned. Hendrik and Willow stood in front of the wall filled with vials.

"This might be more difficult than we thought," Willow muttered.

Examining the labels on the wall, Tam furrowed her brow. "114, 121, 207. How will we know which one?" Her heart sank. How would they find the serum? They couldn't possibly test everything. "The book ..."

"What did you say?" Willow asked.

"The book. Maybe it says something about the location of the serum." Bending down, Tam unzipped her pack and pulled out the notebook, set it on the dusty countertop, and flipped to the entry under May 24th. It was the part that talked about giving the hogs the modified serum with the added adrenaline. To her dismay, nowhere did it mention the number the serum was filed under. She looked again, turning the next page, looking for clues, but found nothing. It could be any one of those vials on the wall.

"Any numbers at all in there?" Hendrik asked.

Tam shook her head. "No, none. Just the dates above the entries as if that matters."

"Wait, what did you say?"

"I said there are no numbers anywhere."

"Except the dates though, right?"

"Yeah . . ."

"Well look at these." He pointed to the labels. "323 could be March 23rd and 414 could be April 14th."

Tam flipped back to the page she'd been on. "Hey, you may be on to something."

"What's the date they gave them the serum?" Hendrik asked.

"May 24th."

"So that would be 524."

Willow stooped down. "Number 524. This must be it." Carefully, she slid out the tray. "Three vials left. Is that enough?"

Shrugging, Tam wrapped each vial in brown paper before placing them in her pack. "It will have to be. I hope you're right about the dates, Hendrik."

As they made their way back to the front entrance, Tam froze. While they'd been in the lab, the conditions outside had changed. Kapros had filled the path in front of the building. They would need to find another way out. So far, the boar hadn't seen her. She took several steps backward and tripped over Willow's foot.

"Ow," she yelped. "What's wrong?" Willow looked up just in time to see a ragged boar with half an ear turn toward them. It let out an excited squeal, alerting the other pigs. They turned to run, falling over Hendrik, just as a loud crash sounded behind them. The animals had broken through.

"What's going-" Hendrik gasped, scrambling to his feet. They ran back to the stairwell, slamming it behind them just as something rammed the door. "Keep climbing," Tam urged. She ventured a look over her shoulder and regretted it. The head of a kapros was jammed in the doorway, eyes darting wildly, his snout bloodied from his frantic pursuit. Continuing to race up the stairs, she heard another series of crashes. They kept climbing until they came to the roof.

Hendrik slammed the door and heaved a sigh of relief. "We should be safe up here."

Walking to the edge of the roof, Tam gazed down. The building was completely surrounded. The noise had drawn kapros from all over the city.

Willow stood by her side. "Now what?"

Tam took off her pack and held up the serum. She raised her eyebrows.

Hendrik took a step back. "No … no way. We don't know what it's going to do."

Biting her lip, Tam swirled the amber colored liquid. "All the more reason to test it before we get back to Aviary."

"She has a good point," Willow said.

Hendrik looked down at the kapros, then back at the serum. He ran his fingers through his hair before throwing his hands up. "Yeah, okay. Let's do it."

"Now you're talking." Tam took the cap off the vial and held it over the edge.

"*Whoa, whoa*. Can't just do it that way. Here." Hendrik handed her a piece of smoked pheasant. "Put a few drops on this."

"Right. Do you think a few drops is enough?"

"We can always try more if it doesn't work."

After placing three drops on the meat, she lifted it toward Willow and Hendrik. "Let's do it together."

Nodding, they each grabbed hold. With solemn looks on their faces, they held it over the ledge. "Ready? Three, two, one …" As they released the bird and watched it fall, it disappeared amid the throng of crazed animals below. They waited in silence for several moments.

Willow tilted her head and perched on the edge of the overhang. "How long do you think until we know if it worked?"

Tam shrugged. "I don't know. The notebook doesn't really say. Maybe we should've added more."

A shrill squeal rang out above the rest. Tam held her hands over her ears and searched the crowd. Below, the kapros were backing away, forming a circle around the hog making the horrible racket. It flailed around, convulsing like it was having a seizure. Even from their height, she could see foam dripping from its mouth, forming a puddle on the ground.

Hendrik swallowed. "I think it's ... I think it's growing."

He was right. As they watched, the creature swelled and expanded like a balloon. The other kapros kept backing away. Finally, when it was more than twice as big and seemed it would burst, it lay still.

"It's like, a mega-boar now," Hendrick whispered in awe. A brave hog ventured closer, sniffing the ground near the beast. Tam held her breath as she waited to see what would happen next. Would it really turn on the others, or had they made things worse by creating a super beast?

"I think we killed it." Willow frowned.

Maybe she was right. Tam could no longer see the chest rising and falling. The other kapros had gained more confidence. The ring was starting to close in as they surrounded the body, no doubt hungry for the fresh meat of the dead animal. Just when it looked like they were ready to pounce, the mega-boar leapt to its feet and sunk his teeth into the closest kapros, tearing it in two. It didn't stop there. Ignoring the remains of the hog, it pounced on another, flinging the body to the side as it tore out a sizable chunk from its neck. The kapros were squealing and grunting in panic now, running over each other in a race to get away. The mega-boar gave chase, tearing and shredding as it went, leaving a trail of blood and various body parts in its path.

The creature's taste for blood was insatiable. It gobbled and snapped, its belly expanding. It must have killed dozens without slowing. Tam marveled at how much the animal's stomach could hold. *How much longer could it keep this up?* The stomach finally became so large, its legs gave out. Still, it continued on, pulling itself on its belly and grabbing the bodies it had left behind as it went. This thing wasn't going to stop, and its stomach looked ready to burst.

Willow shielded her eyes from the sun. "Guys, I think it's going to—"

A dull, thunderous rumble cut off her words, followed by a gush like a muddy waterfall landing on a bed of rocks as bits of kapros, and its own innards rained down all around the creature.

Tam blinked and looked at the others. They stood with their mouths open and a look of shock in their eyes. She blinked again. "Well, that was unexpected."

With the area surrounding them now free of kapros, they made their way back down the steps and through the town, careful to avoid the chunks of boar guts littering the streets. The stench made Tam heave. She raised her shirt over her mouth and nose to block the smell as they walked on. Thankfully, the commotion seemed to scare away all the kapros in the surrounding area. They made it back to the tree line without seeing a single one. As they approached the forest, a shape dropped in front of them.

"Jacob!" Willow exclaimed. A smile spreading across her face. "Thank you for saving me back there." She made a move to hug him, but he sprang back as if she were a viper.

Willow held up her hands. "No touching. Got it. Sorry."

He pointed back toward the city with a bewildered expression. "What made the boar kill the other boar?"

"We have a special serum," Tam tried to explain.

He tilted his head. "A serum?"

Tam tried again. "A drink. We have a drink that makes boar kill each other."

He nodded, his eyes bright with wonder. "Well, well, well. You be smart too!"

Tam grinned. "With your help."

"Guys," Hendrik motioned to them from the edge of the forest. "We really need to get back. Who knows how long we have until the village is destroyed."

With a wave and a call of farewell, Willow turned to follow Hendrik, but Tam hesitated. She took a step toward Jacob. "You should come with us. There are others. You don't have to be alone."

Jacob shook his head. "No. This be my home. My kingdom. Besides, Pricilla would never forgive me," he said, then threw his head back in a fit of laughter.

Tam placed her hand on his shoulder. He flinched but didn't move away. After a second, he put his hand on her shoulder too. "Goodbye, Jacob. And thanks again for everything. Hopefully we'll see you again, friend."

"Goodbye ... friend," Jacob said, then spun around and dashed on all fours back toward the city. She watched after him for a moment, then ran to join the others.

Excited by the results of the day, they made their way back toward Aviary twice as fast. It was growing dark, but there was a full moon with a clear sky, so they continued on, anxious to share their discovery. Tam nearly missed a jump in the failing light. As they paused to catch their breath, Willow rested her head against a branch. Somehow, she had mastered the skill of taking a power nap while balanced precariously in a tree.

Tam sat back and took a long swig of water from her canteen.

Hendrik glanced at her from the corner of his eye. "We should be back in less than an hour. How are you holding up? How's your arm?"

"Oh, good, I think." She'd been so high on adrenaline, the dull ache had gone by unnoticed, but the wound seemed to have reopened. The makeshift bandage was nearly soaked through.

"Better let me rebandage it. Don't want the smell of fresh blood drawing in any kapros."

She nodded and began to unwrap the cloth. Hendrik lifted his shirt so he could rip another piece off. Tam blushed and held out her hand. "It's all right. I think I've got something in my pack I can use. Besides, I wouldn't want you to get cold."

"Cold? Are you kidding? All this climbing has me sweating like a kapros."

Tam handed him a rag. "Still, you can use this. No need to rip up that stylish half-shirt you got there."

Hendrik glanced down at his exposed stomach beneath the tear in his shirt and grinned. "Ah yes, I'm such a trendsetter. Might have been nice to have this cloth in the first place."

Tam rolled her eyes. "I was a little distracted what with the bleeding all over and whatnot the first time."

Gingerly, as if her arm might shatter, Hendrik wrapped her arm back up. "There, that should be better."

"What, no kiss this time?"

"Well, if you insist ..." Hendrick leaned forward, lips in an exaggerated pucker.

"Ew, no." She shoved his face back.

"Ouch! You almost made me fall."

Tam laughed. "Don't be so dramatic."

Hendrik leaned back, gazing up at the leaves. "This is nice. I'm glad you don't hate me anymore."

"Who said I don't?" Tam raised her eyebrows. When he didn't respond, she leaned back and looked up too. The colors were already starting to change. I would be autumn soon. A gust of wind sent several leaves spiraling to the ground. "I'm glad too," she said after a moment.

"Yeah?"

"Yes, I'm glad we're friends." She reached out and caught a leaf in her hand, and her eyes met Hendrik's.

"Is that all we are? Friends?"

Tam lowered her gaze. "What more do you want?" she snapped, then bit her tongue. *What was wrong with her?* That wasn't meant to sound so harsh. "Sorry," she mumbled, dusting off her hands. "I know I'm horrible company. And you ..." Tam dropped her voice so quiet it was barely audible. "You deserve better."

"What was that?"

She shook her head. "Nothing. We should keep moving. I haven't seen any kapros in a while and that worries me. If they aren't in the forest, they might be attacking again. Who knows what Aviary looks like now."

He nodded as if snapping out of a stupor. "Right, yeah, let's go."

"Willow, come on." Tam gave her a nudge, and the girl jumped, nearly toppling over.

"I'm awake," Willow said with a yawn.

Tam put her climbing claws back on, preparing to move on. She stopped when Hendrik placed a hand on her shoulder. "Sticks."

"What?"

"There isn't anyone better." He smiled and leapt forward to the next tree.

Tam's face burned. So, he had heard her. How embarrassing. She tried to ignore her rapid heartrate as she followed him. It must be elevated from trying to keep their quick pace, that's all it was.

They'd just started to fall into a good rhythm when they stopped again at a large clearing. She didn't remember this being here before.

"Hendrik, how much farther to Aviary?" Even in the moonlight, she could tell that his face had gone pale. "Hendrik?"

"This is Aviary."

Chapter Twenty

Tam's heart felt like it was beating in her throat. "What do you mean this is Aviary?"

"I mean, this is it. Or was it. Look down."

Her breathing grew hoarse as she stared at what was left of Aviary. Fallen trees, crushed houses, and various unrecognizable pieces of what was left of the city were strewn across the forest. "Dad, Gran ..." she whispered and dropped to the ground, running full speed. There was no time to lose by making her way around the remaining tree line on either side. Not waiting to see if her friends were following her, she kept running.

Up ahead, a large swarm of kapros were ramming the trees, trying to knock the platforms and homes down. Her heart leapt with hope. There was something left of the city after all. Using her grappler, Tam didn't even slow down as she aimed it up toward the trees and fired. The line zipped her up with great speed, and her feet grazed the confused boars as she sped over them and up to the nearest platform.

The kapros were everywhere, ramming and pushing the trees below. The floor shook as she hurried toward her home, dreading what she might find. Trees were down here and there, making the journey trickier than usual. Tam had to use her grappler in places where the bridges had been knocked down. Finally, her home came into view. It was still standing if not a little crooked. She glanced into the enclosure while running by. The bird food was scattered all over the ground, and the birds were diving down and filling themselves. They were glad for the extra food and completely unbothered by the shaking trees. She came to her home and threw open the door.

"Dad? Gran? Where are you?"

"Up here," came Dad's voice. Dashing up the stairs, she found him sitting on Gran's bed, holding her hand in his. When he saw Tam, he jumped up and embraced her. "Oh Tamerelda. When I couldn't find you, I thought ... I thought the worst. So many have been killed."

Tam tore herself away, tears in her eyes. "Dad, listen. You need to get out of here. It's not safe."

Gran's eyes were wild. "The kapros. The kapros will kill us all!"

"I can't. I won't leave Gran to die," Dad said. "She isn't strong enough to make it to the caves." A crash shook the home, causing the room to tilt.

"Is that where everyone is? At the caves?"

"No, only the strongest. Most of those who remained are in their homes waiting to die. They were either too weak to travel or refused to leave a family member behind. Some of the Pathfinders stayed behind in a last attempt to lure the kapros away, but I don't know what became of them."

"Listen to me, Dad. There's still hope. Take Gran to the big tree in the center of town. "My friends and I have a plan."

"What plan?" Another crash sent Tam sprawling. Dad helped her to her feet.

"Never mind. There's no time to explain. Go!"

Her father nodded and bent down, scooping the frail old woman into his arms. Tam held the door for him and helped him down the stairs as the house lurched dangerously.

Once out the door, Tam gave him a final kiss on the cheek and watched him make his way toward the great tree.

"Tam!" Willow called, jumping down and landing next to Tam. Hendrik was just behind her.

"Guys, we need to get to the smokehouse to get some more meat."

Hendrik nodded. "Lead the way."

Tam opened the enclosure where the birds were still greedily gobbling up the birdseed and unzipped her pack just as another tremor shook the trees. She fell to the floor, dropping her bag. It rolled to the other side of the cage. As Hendrik retrieved the bag, Tam stood, and together, they made their way to the smokehouse shed in the back of the enclosure.

There were only three pieces of meat left. That would have to do for now.

"Here." She handed one to Hendrik and one to Willow, keeping the last one for herself. Reaching into the bag, Tam noticed a vial was missing, but there was no time to worry about that now. She splashed several drops on each piece, then placed the remaining serum in a cabinet.

"Alright. Let's end this."

As they ran out, Hendrik caught Tam's hand in his. "In case we don't make it, I ..."

Tam leaned forward and kissed Hendrik's lips then stepped back and smiled at the look of surprise on his face. "Me too," she said.

He regained his composure in an instant. "I was just going to say, nice working with you," he said with a wink.

Tam grinned and rolled her eyes. With no time to lose, she raced to the nearest edge. A fight was raging below. Several Pathfinders were locked into a losing battle. A man was ripped in two right before her eyes. His screamed echoed above the grunts. Feeling sick, she tore her gaze away. Not wanting to waste her only piece of pheasant, she made her way closer to be certain it would be ingested by a kapros.

As Tam made her way toward the ground, she spotted Cassia riding on the back of one of the boars. The commander struck its neck and used her grappler to swing back to the safety of the trees as it toppled over. Cassia didn't stay there long. In an instant, she was back on the ground, dodging and stabbing another kapros in the heart with her blade. It was impressive to watch.

However, Cassia was severely outnumbered and only a fraction of the Pathfinders were left. They couldn't hold out much longer. Cassia was surrounded. She shot her grappler to the nearest tree, but while zipping forward, a kapros snapped onto her leg. She screamed in pain.

"No!" Tam shouted, temporarily drawing the boar's attention. With her hand outstretched, her focus was so completely on the battle, she didn't see the kapros about to ram the tree. It shook with a tremendous crash, throwing Tam off balance. She fell with a gasp, headfirst over the side, hitting the ground with a thud, and her lungs gasping for air.

Rolling behind a stump, Tam sat up and searched for her commander. Cassia was several hundred feet away, still in the jaws of the hulking beast. Could she make it in time? Jumping to her feet, she half ran, half stumbled toward them, swinging blindly and hoping to confuse and anger the creature enough to release its prey. Her blade connected, and the beast swung toward her with an angry snort. Cassia hung limply from the kapros's mouth.

It was too late. With a scream of rage, she flew at the creature, hacking and slashing. The creature flung Cassia to the side and rose up to its full height. Tam swallowed and took a step back. The creature swung his tusks, knocking the blade from her hand. The beast's eyes gleamed as a trickle of blood rolled down its face from where her shoka had glanced off. She backed up further until a row of sharp branches poked into her back from a fallen tree, stopping her retreat. Trapped.

Letting out a deafening squeal, the kapros charged toward her. With the branches on either side blocking her escape, Tam made a swift decision and dove toward the creature's feet. It shot over her and plunged into the log. She scrambled forward and retrieved her sword, but when she spun around, the creature was still. It had died standing in place, pierced like a stuck pig on the row of branches. Red pooled below it, coating the ground and standing out against the brown and green foliage around it.

Tam's hands shook as she raced to Cassia. The commander lay motionless, eyes closed, blood seeping from the wounds in her leg and side. To Tam's surprise, she was still breathing. The breaths came in labored heaves, but they still came. Grabbing the woman under the arms, she pulled her behind a large stump, out of view of the battle.

"Commander?"

Cassia's eyes flickered open. "Tam? What ... what are you doing here?"

Tam put her arm under the woman's neck. "Commander! It's okay. Everything is going to be fine. Hendrik, Willow and I found a way to stop this. To put an end to it all."

"Then go. What are you waiting for? There are people waiting. People who need—" Cassia's eyes began to close as Tam frantically tried to press her hands against the gaping wound in her commander's side, but it was no use. The injury was too great for Tam's limited skills.

"Commander? Commander Cassia? No ... not you. Not you too."

"Go," Cassia murmured. Tam felt the woman's muscles relax as she breathed her last breath, then lay still.

Tam put some leaves under Cassia's head then let it rest back on the ground. Angry tears leapt to her eyes. She would stop this. She had to. For Cassia, for Dover, and all those whose lives ended too soon because of these creatures. Gritting her teeth, she set her jaw and stood.

Tam reached for her pack that held the meat coated with the formula and froze. Her pack? Where was her pack? It must have dropped to the ground when she fell. Peering around the stump, she saw it. It was under a tree right near where she'd suspected. To get to it, she would have to get past several kapros. Gritting her teeth and picking up her shoka, Tam took a deep breath. Time to put those stealth skills to use again.

She sprinted from one tree to the next. The pack was between her and a group of kapros. Crouching down, she inched forward, eyes trained on the ground to prevent tripping over a fallen limb. Her head bumped into something firm, stopping her progress. A tree? Slowly, her eyes drifted up. Not a tree but the furry leg of a kapros matted with blood. A drop of something warm and slimy splashed on her hand. She lifted her head higher. The drooling jaws of a kapros hovered above. Scrambling backward, she watched in dismay as another boar snatched up her bag and began ripping it to shreds, flinging the contents all over the forest.

Tam leapt to her feet and ran for the nearest tree, gasping as she tripped over a raised root. Holding out her blade, she spun around to face the heaving animal. It scraped the ground with its hoof and lowered its head. When the creature charged, she took careful aim. Just before being crushed, Tam stood and plunged the blade upward. The kapros slammed into her, taking her breath away.

When she opened her eyes, the body of the now dead monster was on top of her, pinning down her legs. Grabbing the hilt of the blade, she tugged, but it was stuck. Another boar appeared over the top of the fallen one. Reaching back, her fingers felt for an arrow. Only one remained. The rest must have fallen out sometime during the struggle. The creature lunged just as she brought her arm forward, plunging the arrow into its eye. It squealed and fell backward, twitching. With a grunt of effort, Tam scooted up a little further. If only she could get to her grappler, but it was pinned under the beast too.

A group of kapros spotted her. Tam tried to kick with all her might, but her legs remained stuck. As they snapped their jaws and ran forward, anxious to get to the easy kill first, many thoughts ran through her head. Things she regretted saying or doing. But mostly, to her surprise, she felt at peace. The serum would work. It was only a matter of time, and everyone would be saved. Even after losing her piece of pheasant, Hendrick and Willow still had theirs. No matter what happened to her, this would make Mom and Dad proud. Their mission had been a success. Gritting her teeth, she prayed the end would come quick.

A loud squeal made the kapros stop dead in their tracks. Tam opened her eyes just in time to see a mega-boar snatch up one of the beasts and fling it to the side while the others ran in terror. Its eyes went to her next. It ran forward, snatching the kapros that had been pinning her legs as if it were a doll. Grabbing her freed grappler from the ground, she took a wild shot. It caught on something and pulled her upward. The mega-boar snapped his jaws as she flew by, barely missing her feet.

She landed against a tree with a thud, smacking the side of her head. With a throbbing headache, Tam lowered herself down, finding a foothold on the platform below. Her legs gave out beneath her. She winced and slid to the floor, watching the sight below. It was a complete bloodbath. Kapros were running and squealing, trying to get away from the three huge mega-boar that had ingested the serum. Hers must have been eaten after all. After a while, they all disappeared into the distance, and Tam heard the rumbling gush of a giant's end. It was crazy to think that the same serum that killed so many humans was now their salvation.

Tam's ankle throbbed, and she wasn't sure if it would hold her weight. Closing her eyes in exhaustion, she lay against the tree. She wasn't sure how much time had gone by before Hendrik appeared. His face was as white as ash, and blood dripped from a gash above his eyebrow.

"Tam, I've been looking for you! Are you okay? I lost sight of you in the commotion."

"I'm okay. I think I might have sprained my ankle though. I can't walk."

"Let's get you to the town center. All the injured are being treated there." He helped her gingerly to her feet, wrapping an arm around her waist. As they hobbled along, even though she was in pain, Tam couldn't stop smiling. They had done it. They had actually done it.

"Your dad will be proud, Tam."

Tam leaned into Hendrik, feeling the warmth of his chest on her face. "So will your sisters. Are they okay?"

Hendrik was beaming. "Yes, the kapros hardly touched the trees near our home. They're okay. They're all okay."

Tam reached up, touching Hendrik's cheek. "I'm so glad."

Town center was not only still standing, it was bustling with activity. Her dad rushed forward when he saw Tam. He embraced her, tears falling down his face.

"Are you okay? What happened out there? Why did the attacks suddenly stop?"

"I'm okay, just a sprain. And it's a long story."

"Come. Tell me while they get you bandaged up." He put Tam's other arm around his neck as they hobbled along.

Everyone around them still seemed in shock. Many were looking for loved ones.

Dad and Hendrik helped her sit on a log to wait her turn getting bandaged up.

"I'll be right back," Dad said. "I need to check on your grandma."

"Tell her the serum worked," Tam said with a grin.

"The what?"

"She'll know."

Dad shrugged and turned to walk away. Just over his shoulder, Tam caught a glimpse of several familiar faces. She was relieved to see her friend, Elnor, and her family helping at the medic station.

Willow was getting a cut on her leg cleaned. A rush of relief flooded Tam. She almost ran to her before remembering her hurt leg.

"Tam! Hendrik!" Willow jumped up and ran to them instead. They all clung together for several moments in a group hug, laughing with relief.

"I can't believe it's over," Willow said after they had let go.

"I know," Tam said then dropped her eyes. "Commander Cassia didn't make it."

"No ..." Willow whispered.

Tam's eyes stung. She wiped a tear away. "Cassia died fighting. She was a hero."

Willow shook her head. "So many dead. So much to rebuild. And what if they attack again?"

Hendrik balled up his fist. "If they do, we'll be ready with the serum."

"Wait. The serum," Tam said.

"What are you talking about? You left them in the shed, right?"

"No. One of the vials fell out, and I didn't have time to look for it. We should go get it. We need to conserve every bit we can."

"But your leg," Hendrik objected.

"There are far worse injuries than mine that should be seen first anyway. We'll be right back. Do you guys mind?"

Hendrik and Willow each put one of her arms around their shoulders to helped her walk. They weaved their way back between the people, not stopping until they were at the enclosure. Unlatching the door on the netting, Tam couldn't help but notice how quiet it was.

"Where are the birds?" Willow asked.

Tam frowned. "I don't know, but the vial must be on the floor somewhere." She scanned the platform and froze. "I found it."

The vial was on the ground, shattered. The remaining serum was spattered all over what was left of the birdseed. There were still no birds in sight. "Hendrik, you don't think that …"

Swallowing, Hendrik pointed to the net overhead. "Yes, I do."

She followed his gaze to the top of the enclosure. The netting had been shredded to pieces, leaving a gaping hole to the sky.

About the Author

Emily A. Steward spent the better part of her childhood dressed as a ninja and trying to convince others to call her 'Ace'. When she wasn't saving the world from evil samurai, she could usually be found in the branches of a tree reading a good book. She now lives in the Pacific Northwest with her husband, four daughters, and dog Bentley. Though she seldom dresses like a ninja now, her adventurous spirit remains, as does her love of tree climbing and reading good books.

About the Artist

Chad Steward is an elementary school teacher with a passion for art. He has been drawing most of his life and dabbled in many different types of mediums. In his teen years, he became really angsty and only drew anime characters with cool guy poses. In his later years, he diversified and began developing his talent as a graphic artist. Chad also loves llamas and alpacas. When he is not drawing, he's dreaming of petting their delightful fur.

Made in the USA
Columbia, SC
06 July 2024